Ondine
Vol 1 A Cash City Omegaverse Story
Shasta de Leon

Smith Book Investments

Book cover and illustration by Killdera

Copyedit by Cupid's Inkwell

First edition 2025

979-8-9996433-2-2

Contents

Also by Shasta

*To all those who did the
work and found their peace.
The world spins madly on.*

Introduction

The omegaverse is as diverse as the writers who write it. Every author has their own rules when it comes to this speculative fiction world. In mine, the designations do not shift. There are alpha, beta, and omega designations only. Around 80% of the human population is designated beta, while the rest is made up mainly of alphas, with an even smaller population of omegas. Omegas can only get pregnant during their heats, a time of extreme sexual possession, and during their heat, only an alpha partner can satisfy them. I tried to cover most of my lore in the text, so if you have questions, happy reading—

1

The Heat Clinic

Ondine

Tears stream down my face as I stumble onto the street in front of the Omega Heat Clinic. My clothes are askew, and I hope they aren't inside out and backwards. But I can't stop and fix myself even if I wanted to. Although my heat spike is over, it could come back at any time, so I need to get out of here. My hands are shaking so hard, it causes my shoulders to shake too. My jaw is tight, and my skin is fucking hot. As I turn the corner, I can feel Arnold's spent roll down both thighs. He'd come in me only moments prior. I stifle a cry. I can't cry. Not yet. I have to get somewhere safe and quickly.

The closest Heat Clinic is on the other side of the city, at least a forty-minute walk. It's another private clinic, and most likely, it could be full. They don't take walk-ins without a significant cost, and I've already spent all my money for this heat at this clinic.

Omegas don't always have to pay. There are free clinics, but they come with caveats. I'd have to sign long contracts and agree to placement assessments and trials. It is all in good faith. I remind myself that no one wants an unattached omega walking the streets of their city. It's like having a naked woman with a briefcase filled with cash running around batting her eyelashes.

Which was exactly what I was doing (minus the cash), and I was within a few hours from my next heat, and running down the streets of one of the largest ABO (Alpha/Beta/Omega) populated cities in the west.

Arnold's beautiful face appears in my memory, his eyebrows pressed together, anguish written all over him, regret radiating between us.

Oh god, I'm a monster.

Arnold is perfect. And I knew it was a matter of time before he realized I was never worthy of his adoration. His tawny red hair was sweat soaked when his hands raked through it, as he said the most damning words.

"We shouldn't have done that."

I'd gone to the Clinic for my heat spike, but the spike happened too quickly. Too rough. I'd lost my ever-living mind. So when I saw Arnie there, prepping my room with nesting materials, I'd pounced. I'd wanted him for longer than I'm willing to admit.

A beta.

A beta whose job was to make sure I had what I needed in the Clinic I was paying for. It was his job to make sure I had everything I needed for my heat. To have the alpha males to satiate my sex crazed body. To have the food and water I needed for the several days I'd be in that state. It was his job to adjust my nesting materials rental order to my taste. It was his job to check in on me. To answer questions. To assign alphas.

And yet my stupid omegabrain took it all wrong. He made me feel special. He made me feel like the only omega there. The only omega he wanted to care for. And when the heat spike rammed through my body like a live wire.

I wanted him inside me.

I turn another corner, passing a few unattached alpha males who turn all the way around to stare at me. My pheromones are potent. I look up in time to see the men sneer, smelling Arnie on me, most likely. I just hope they won't follow me.

Omegas are uncommon. Unattached omegas running through the city covered in *come fuck me* pheromones and the spent of a male fresh on their skin—uncommon and dangerous as all hell.

Plus, there have been two missing omegas in the news this week.

It's not like an alpha would want to hurt an omega, but their instinct to claim would overpower any sense. And if there was anything significant about my scent to them, they wouldn't be able to stop themselves.

I doubt I'd be able to deter a 250 pound man made of pure muscle, being ruled by primal instincts. Alphas are larger than everyone around them. Usually well above 6 feet tall. They are always dealing with so much testosterone that they need to be physical, and they've got the muscles and power for it. Also, most alphas have personality traits that make them aggressive, and let's just say it—narcissists.

Uncaring assholes.

Omegas usually have handlers or hire protection to keep them safe. They don't go running around the city practically in heat, all alone. Anything can happen.

Even I couldn't say no to my instincts. Arnie is strictly forbidden from touching the omegas he cares for. All of the special treatment he'd given me—or at least a lot of it—could be explained as part of his duties, except for what we just did. What I made him do.

Arnie is a beta. What 80% of the population's designation is. He's a regular man. Omegas are only supposed to be with alphas. It's pretty much a law. Well, it's not actually a law, but there are enough laws adjacent to make it one.

A fully formed pack is outside of criticism and social norms. "Stay out of their nest" is the saying. They can do what they want in their pack. But even then, a female omega and a male beta—it's as taboo as it comes.

We are only for alphas.

I reach the entrance for the underground train and decide that getting to the other clinic is more important than the chance of running into any unhinged alphas down here. I dart down the cement steps and slide my card for entrance. My satchel flips around my body to my back as I run to catch the train that just arrived. I'd never even taken it off while Arnie rutted into me on the floor of my unmade nest, in my assigned room, with the door wide open.

Remembering what I have in my bag, I stop suddenly and whip the bag around to my front, reaching in for the scent-blocking spray. The little bottle has some weight to it, as if it has plenty of juice left. I tip my head back and look up to the sky, thanking whoever may be up there for this small mercy. Tears glaze over my eyes.

The train doors screech open, and before I can blink away the tears, I hop onto the train. There's no missing it and having to wait for the next one. I don't have the time.

Just as the doors close behind me, the train starts up. But it isn't going west. The train slides across the tracks, headed east.

"Fuck!" I yell at myself, causing a few people around me to dart their eyes in my direction. I bow my head in apology and turn away.

Fuck. Fuck Fuck. Fuck.

Wrong train!

There's this growing heat in my chest, and it's spreading through my body. It's an early sign of a heat spike. The next sign is my fucking pussy slicking.

I grab onto a bar to hold myself steady. My right hand is still in my bag, clutching the scent blocker.

Think, Ondine. Think! I command myself to be present. To be human for just a little longer. If I go into heat on this train, someone will call Emergency Services, right? And then they will take me to a state-owned Omega Clinic. They will probably pump me full of suppressants and hormones to get this to stop. But I am already full of hormones and suppressants that the Heat Clinic gives me. What if it hurts me? What if it's just the right chemical cocktail to turn me into a drooling vegetable?

And what if they are looking for me right now? If Arnie called the authorities on me for assaulting him, would I even go to a Clinic? Or would they just take me to jail to die in a holding cell?

Halfway in my head, and halfway actually present on this train, it's surprising I notice him. A tall blonde alpha male in a gray-blue suit turns his whole head in my direction. He's holding the bar above his head. His serene gray eyes look me up and down, and his head cocks to one side. A silent question on his slightly parted lips. I just caught the attention of an alpha.

He's going to smell me.

And I am a beacon calling any available alpha to rut into me right on this dirty train floor.

I shove my hand back into my bag and clasp around the scent blocker. I turn around in a few circles until I find an open seat and fall into it. At the same time, I'm trying to think where this train is going. It was red, right? The light had been red over the door. The red line goes across town, only a few stops, making it the express. Its last stop is the Clinic at Castell Square Garden, but going the other direction—my eyes close and my head drops in despair.

Oh, no.

This train goes out of the city, under the river. To the suburbs on the peninsula. There's no clinic there. I could get off at the next stop, but I know as soon as I think this, the next stop is under the river and is 30 minutes away. It's going to take me at least 90 minutes to get to the Clinic. Will I have another spike in 90 minutes?

I feel the air shift over me, so I open my eyes and peek up. Staring at the alpha with the gray eyes, I realize my head has been bowed in deference. Like I am submitting. His big grin confirms that's exactly what I looked like. I swallow my fear, pull out the scent blocker, pop off the cap, face the nozzle towards me, but before I can press down, his hand shoots out to stop me.

"One second. I need another second to enjoy your scent before you take it away," he says with a voice that could melt an iceberg.

My eyes go wide, and I just know my pupils dilate. If I didn't know any better, I'd say this man used his alpha voice on me.

I pause and let him take me in.

What else can I do except let him?

Being an omega means being at the mercy of someone else's needs and desires at all fucking times. And I'm good at accepting its outcomes. I expect its unpredictability. I expect that nothing will go how I want it. For example, I want to get to another clinic, and yet, here I am, on the wrong train, with an alpha standing above me, his eyes closed, and he breathes me in. And why do I expect everything to go to shit?

Because it always does.

Otherwise, I wouldn't be a fucking omega to begin with.

His watch matches his shoes and belt with black leather and silver trimmings. He's well put together. His leather satchel is like a compliment to mine. His hand is still over mine, with the scent-blocker in my loose fist. All the hair on my body rises to meet this man.

I've only been an omega for one year. I'd say the attention I get from alphas is new, but it's really not. I've always been smaller than my beta friends. My eyes have always been larger and strange. I have a voice that doesn't get shrill or loud. Even when I lose control, it's quiet. I don't feel it matches my inner life, my inner voice, at all.

I wear my hair short; I don't like it on my neck. It's solidly blonde. While I've been skinny my whole life, once I perfumed, my body changed. My breasts grew, and my legs, ass, and hips got some shape. It's a new feeling, so I usually wear oversized clothes. I don't know what to do with this new body. I've never known an omega, so I can't ask. Both my parents were alphas, making me an anomaly.

I catch a whiff of the strange alpha above me, his scent going right to all my senses—birthday cake. He smells like a birthday cake, burning candles and all. I try to move my hand away from him. He holds on for a second longer and then lets go.

He takes a step away, looks around, ensuring no one else is bothering us, and then nods to me. Giving me permission to spray myself. I don't hesitate. I spray myself from top to bottom and then back up again.

He looks like he might pout.

"Pity you had to hide that delicious scent of yours, Omega."

I know it should bother me that he called me by my designation, but being seen for what I am pleases me. Or rather, pleases that innate, primal part of me.

"Where are you headed to? You seem in a hurry," he asks and leans in a little closer, invading my personal space again.

The sway of the car racing along the tracks unsettles my already frayed nerves.

He won't hurt me, I don't think. There's a train car full of people surrounding us. Not directly. The surrounding seats are empty.

"I just needed to get away," I answer.

I have to be careful because most alphas can smell a lie, especially a lie from an omega. Or so the myth says. Maybe that's just something from tv shows.

He considers the answer, then asks, "From the male you were just with?"

I drop my head, and again, it looks like an act of submission. I don't mean to, it's just his eyes are so focused on me, I need to be released.

"Yes," I answer pitifully.

I'd made Arnie participate in a forbidden act. He's most likely lost his job and his reputation. He was good at what he did at the Clinic, and I ruined his life with one sordid mistake.

"My name is Jake Meier. Pack lead of the Meier Pack." Jake extends his hand to me, and I look back up at him, not quite meeting his gray eyes.

I take his hand, its size alarming. The omega side of me is so happy to have my hand in his. Especially so close to my heat. I need an alpha to help me through my heat. Nothing else will help.

And this one smells like birthday cake.

"Ondine." I give him my name. Most omegas drop their surname unless they are attached to a pack. If I were in his pack, even temporarily, I would call myself Meier.

I realize I've been holding my breath when I suddenly gasp for air. He tightens his hold on me.

"You're very pretty, Ondine. Beautiful face. Delicate hands. I bet you're a really good omega."

A knee-jerk reaction to whine at his praise erupts from me. The only thing I can do is not make it so loud. I hope only Jake hears it. His smile spreads across his face, revealing a Cheshire Cat-sized grin.

I crave this man's attention, and I want to reject that instinct.

I am a bad omega.

Images of Arnie, desperate, colored red, and bleary-eyed, flash through my mind. What I did to him. Being told I am a good omega, by even a stranger, is what everything in me is craving after I fucked up so badly.

"You know, Ondine," he pauses, so he can enjoy my reaction to hearing my name on his lips, "My pack is seeking an omega companion. I was just in the city today for my formal interview for placement at the Institute. This may be kismet."

I'm not sure I hear him right. I drop my jaw as I try to discern if I heard him correctly.

"Seeking an omega?"

"We've never had one. It's been the three of us for a while now, but my pack mate, Shadow, he's not doing well. I want to make him happy. Shadow is a unique alpha. He's good, but a bit needy. I think an omega would satisfy his needs that Sebastian and I can't meet."

Alphas can be with whomever they want, disregarding designation, I think bitterly. But it's a mark of power and prestige to have an omega, but that doesn't mean they can't fuck whoever they please.

Even betas.

An alpha can fuck a beta, and it would mean very little. So, is this more than fucking?

"Oh," is all I manage to say.

The train makes its descent to the underground rail. The lights dim, leaving only red and blue track lights on the ceiling. Shadows casting all over us.

"Would you like to come and meet them?" Jake says with his honey-toned voice. "I can show you the contract we've already made. We can do this privately, without the Institute's involvement. Come meet my pack, baby."

This was too much to take in at once. He is presenting me with all sorts of details and scenarios. Again, I find myself on the way to solving my problems, even when presented with an unforeseen detour. It's been the only thing I can expect in life—the now.

If the day ever came when I made plans and got to see them through, I'd be more shocked than I'd ever been with these wrenches.

I nod my head, afraid of my own voice.

He smiles brighter, and there is a gleam in his eyes. The red light reflects in his bright eyes and casts shadows across his face. My body floods with oxytocin at having pleased an alpha. Shit, that's going to make me spike.

He releases my hand, and I lean back, hold my satchel to my chest, and close my eyes. Determined to meditate in order to hold off on a spike, at least until I meet the other members of the Meier Pack.

I'm too close to my heat to make decisions using logic. As evident by what I just did to Arnie.

We don't speak for the rest of the journey. I don't ask more about his pack or himself, and he doesn't even seem curious in return. He seems satisfied with his accomplishment. That solving the problem of choosing an omega was gratifying. He takes up a defensive pose around me. Facing towards the other passengers, his legs wide, and his eyes on any potential threats. I'm grateful for it, even if I should be alarmed. I don't know him from Adam.

2

Run, Ondine. Run!

Ondine

We arrive at the end of the line, the lights return, and the train comes to a complete stop. Jake gestures for me to follow. I fall in step behind him without trouble. The platforms come together at a point, and Jake turns towards the parking structure, and I just stop.

Can I really do this? This is the end of the line. The train will head back under the river, back to the city, and across town, all the way to another Heat Clinic. Maybe I should just get back on the train?

Jake notices I'm not with him and turns around. Fifteen feet separate us. He cocks his head to the side, asking, *Are you coming?*

"I'm going into heat," I confess into the space between us. "Any time now."

He nods in understanding.

"Then let's get you home."

I need a home. I need an alpha who can make me come.

A lot.

I have no choice here. This has to happen. Blinking rapidly, my eyes clear and look around me. No one is around.

He prowls up to me and takes my elbow in his hand and leads me away.

His car is parked at the very top of the parking structure next to the station. It's a two-seater sports car. Silver with a bluish hue. I climb into the passenger seat, sinking into the leather. He turns on the heated seats, and it wretches another whine from me.

"That's such a beautiful sound, baby," he groans and then adjusts himself in the seat next to me.

His car is saturated in his birthday cake scent. Indicating he's probably the only one who drives this car. I have the errant thought that I don't have anything of Arnie's with me. Nothing with his smell. Betas don't have potent scents like alphas or omegas, but an article of clothing would still "smell" like Arnie. His unique man smell.

I wish I'd taken something of his with me today. I'd left anything of him behind.

It's a fifteen minute drive to the Meier Pack home, even though it's just a few miles. It's in a closed neighborhood on a peninsula on the river. Trees surround his property, and there's a dock out back. It's got a witch's hat turret and a wrap-around porch. It's actually a beautiful home. I note the fleet of black SUVs on a driveway next to the house. My breaths are coming in and out more shallow, and a sheen of sweat breaks out over my skin.

Please, god, don't be having another spike.

Jake parks his car in a garage with several other cars and vehicles already inside. Once he turns off the engine, he leans back and breathes in deeply.

"That scent blocker is finally wearing off, baby," he mutters, mostly to himself.

"Alpha Meier," I say, and it makes him shudder.

"Yes, baby?"

I have to be real with myself. I'm fading. Fast.

"I'm running out of time," I whisper. It is so quiet in the car, I don't need to say it any louder for him to hear, anyway.

"You are a good omega, aren't you?" he purrs from his chest, and it goes straight to my pussy.

No, I'm really not.

"Come on, let's get you inside first."

I continue to hold my satchel close to my chest as he directs me into the house from the side door. We get into the kitchen and are greeted by a male beta. Jake excuses him for the day, and the beta is a bit shocked, but does as he says. "And Emmerson," Jake says to him on his way out, "Tell all the other betas to leave the property for now."

There's a note of possession in his voice, and the beta catches it just as clearly as I do. He looks at me with pity and leaves.

That's not great.

What did I get myself into?

3

The Meier Pack

Ondine

"Sebastian! Shadow!" Jake calls up the stairs and then takes me to the piano room.

I don't know what else to call it. It's a corner room with window seats lining the walls and tall windows on two sides. There's a baby grand piano and bookcases on the opposite walls. Through the French doors, two alphas enter.

The first man is large, in every sense of the word. He's a black man with a buzz cut in his tightly curly hair. His light brown skin shines bronze in the sunlight pouring in from the windows, and his beard is short. He has a single gold earring with a sparkling diamond. He looks like he just got done with something physical because he is shiny with sweat and dirt. He has on just a wife-beater, and his jeans are dusty. His arms are enormous. I can't even look him in the face.

"Baby, meet Sebastian," Jake says when my eyes don't wander from his arms.

He nods, a bit confused. "Where have you been, Sabbies? You look run through."

Jake takes in his pack mate from head to toe.

"Emil asked me to help remove that tree trunk by the road. Remember the tree died in the last storm?"

Jake tsks. "Always so helpful."

"Well, we got it."

I look over at the other alpha.

"And this is Shadow," he says.

Shadow, the alpha, they want the omega for. The needy alpha. The different alpha. He's almost like Sebastian's opposite. Pale skin, long black hair knotted at the back of his neck. Dark circles under his eyes. Jake is right about something—Shadow looks a bit ill. He's pretty, though, cut jaw and lovely oil slick black eyes. He's Chinese, I note.

"I'd like you two to meet Odessa. We're considering her for the omega position," Jake says, and I whip my head to look at him.

"My name is Ondine," I correct, hurt leaking into my voice, "On-deen."

"Right, she's about to go into heat."

My mouth hangs open as I turn back to the other two alphas.

Suddenly, my stomach clenches. This is such a fucking bad idea. *But, of course, this would happen when you fuck up as much as I just did.* These are consequences. These alphas are my consequence.

"Interesting," Shadow says, but his tone's neutral.

"Did she come from the Institute?" Sebastian asks.

"I met her on the way home. She's unattached. Thought we could do this privately. Save a middleman."

The two alphas crowd me, pushing me towards Jake until all three surround me. They smell me. The scent-blocker is nearly completely gone at this point.

"She smells like you, and another man, it's strong, like he'd had some sort of intense reaction to her," Sebastian assesses.

"She said she was running away from him," Jake answers, like I am not even here.

I just let them carry on. This is hardly the time or position for me to do anything other than submit and comply.

Doesn't mean I don't fucking hate it.

Shadow ignores them and takes another big breath before saying, "She smells like vanilla and homemade ice cream. Reminds me of the ice cream shop near the academy."

"So you like her then?" Jake asks Shadow earnestly, hoping to solve another problem.

I wonder why they are speaking about me like I'm not here, right in the middle of them.

"Yes, Alpha," Shadow says, and Jake makes a noise that only alphas can make. It's a small rattling noise, for when they are satisfied.

"She needs to sign the contract first," Sebastian tells them.

"Of course, it's on the desk already," Jake gestures to the desk with a folder on it, and I walk over there.

I look back at the alphas. They are young. No one looks like they are yet thirty. I'm only 23, so it's not the worst scenario to be introduced to three alphas not too much older than me. I'd say Sebastian is the oldest, but I could be wrong.

"Go read it, Omega," Sebastian finally addresses me. "It's just for two heats, this one will count even though it's so soon. You'll be paid out before and after. We want your full attention and submission. There's a consideration for extending the contract as well."

I guess I only needed to get Shadow's approval. Not getting Sebastian's open approval as well makes my heart seize. Being an omega is the worst. It makes you crave acceptance from alphas.

I maneuver around the men and go to the desk, sitting on the edge of the chair. I open the envelope and get to reading. They want me to submit, alright. They reserve the right to use an alpha voice on me, only at Jake's prior approval. If I'm favoring one over the other, it's a violation of the contract. I'm to be loyal to them, including their perceived loyalty. I guess that means not speaking with other men. I don't have to cook or clean, a surprising thing. Most packs want their omegas to serve them. I'm guessing the Meier pack has betas for that work.

Then suddenly, I catch something strange—there's a line for me to fill out who my current handler is. It doesn't appear optional.

"Alpha Meier, what does this mean?"

Sebastian walks over to see what I'm pointing at.

"Don't most omegas have handlers? Just write in their name and email." He sounds so no-nonsense.

"I'm a private citizen. I've never had a handler."

He's not wrong. Most omegas have a handler. And some alphas too. It's an important position. They set the rules of courting and ensure they are followed. They keep the person safe. They often live with them and care for them.

Sebastian shrugs.

But there's no option to leave blank. I'm trying to read through the contingencies, but they don't make any sense. I feel the ghost of a cramp, and because I need this to happen, and I have no more time, I write in "self". I slide the document away from me, my fresh signature glistening up at me.

More pain warms my center. "Where will I nest?"

"Just the spare room where you'll be staying is fine."

I close my eyes and refuse to protest. Omegas don't do well nesting where they sleep. But I can't say that. This is what they offered, and I have to take it.

And do I even deserve a fucking nest?

Jake takes the contract from me, adding his signature, and soon it's fully signed.

"You forgot your banking information," Sebastian says as he reviews the contract. I take it back and fill it out, not having looked at the payout. Fuck me. They are offering $20,000 for a signing fee. $80,000 at the contract's end.

What are they paying for? I pay $3,000 for my room at the Heat Clinic. It's exorbitant, but worth it. The alpha partners are well vetted, and the accommodations are outstanding. And there was Arnie.

Don't think about Arnie.

I didn't realize how much money an omega could make on a temporary pack placement. I suppose it's a desirable position. Perhaps if I enrolled in the Institute, I wouldn't have even had this opportunity. They would have chosen another omega. Perhaps, even found an elusive "scent match". Perhaps, she would be an omega who didn't pounce on her crush, the man she'd nearly fallen in love with, demanding he take care of her.

But $100,000. That feels like they are buying more than an omega. "Can I get a copy of this?" I ask. I have to make sure I know what is required of me. Maybe I missed something.

Sebastian smiles at me, and my stomach flips.

"Of course. Let me send this to our lawyer, and I'll email you a copy too."

My email is on the document, so he's got everything he needs.

Jake and Shadow are talking to each other on the other side of the room.

"So I take it the meeting didn't go well?" Shadow asks Jake. Jake looks unhappy and shakes his head no. Are they talking about the interview at the Institute? Jake asked me to do this privately. Is it because they didn't qualify for placement?

No, don't think that. You have a place to hide from your shame and alphas to see you through your heat. Nothing else matters.

Right?

"I guess it worked out. What're the chances of running into an unattached omega on the train? Feels like the beginning of a romance movie."

But the way he says it, it sounds more like the beginning of a much different kind of movie.

***

Sebastian

At least she's pretty. I'll give her that. Does Shadow think she's pretty? I can't tell anymore what he thinks, and what he feels is even more strained.

We'd gotten only through the first step in the application process at the Alpha-Omega Placement Institute, and then we were unceremoniously rejected. We hadn't even gotten an interview or referrals.

We didn't know who or what to blame. But we all looked at Jake, our pack lead, a diagnosed narcissist. It's listed right in his designation registration. While I don't think it would make him a bad alpha to an omega, it's most likely what disqualified us. Ultimately, we didn't get a reason for the rejection. Jake got an appointment with a caseworker to plead our case, but I am guessing it went poorly.

The omega is in the guest room. Hopefully nesting. We were not prepared for this. The house has a place for a nest, but it's used for storage. My eyes twitch just thinking about this situation we are in.

Of course Jake brought home a desperate omega. This is how it would work out for us. We should have just had Jake prowl around the city until he found an omega in the first place.

I don't like it. It feels wrong in some way. We invited a stranger into our home.

But we had to do it. For Shadow.

Shadow needs more than what Jake and I can give him. At first, just our commitment and friendship were enough for him. Our bites and our bonds. But a few years ago, we started to see the changes in him. He sleeps all the time. He hardly eats. I can't even remember the last hobby he had. He watches the same tv shows over and over again. He's been reading the same little pink book for months.

Jake hates problems. And he hates problems in the pack even more.

But nothing he did fixed it.

It was Boone who suggested an omega.

Boone is an alpha and our friend. We'd bond with him, but he's still vetting packs. He was the one who talked to us one night, after we'd been drinking and playing games all night.

I knew that Shadow and Jake started out with a sexual relationship. They met shortly before I came into their lives. But I always thought it was a phase. Something they grew out of. They were just friends and soon pack mates before I even met them.

I guess it was just a few fun nights fucking. And that was all Jake wanted. But Shadow wanted more, and accepted less, it seemed.

I didn't know this until that night, but Shadow also wants me. He wants more than my respect and friendship. But he knows I'm not very open-minded. I didn't mean to reject him, and I don't even remember doing so.

I just think that until a pack is complete, male alpha-alpha relations are not appropriate. That, and I don't want one. I've never felt an attraction for my pack mates. My love for them runs deep, but there is a line for me. Which means—both pack members have rejected Shadow. He is also no longer gaining satisfaction with the betas we have coming in and out of here.

We applied for omega placement shortly after that. I love Shadow. He's my brother and pack mate. However, I can feel him slipping away and becoming less and less himself, and it's not good for anyone.

Our bond is not what it used to be.

Jake claps his hands loudly, getting both of our attention.

"Dina is about to go into heat, so I'll get us out of work for the next few days."

"Ondine—" I correct.

"Yeah, ok. Let's get our business taken care of so we can have some fun." Jake leaves us as he makes his way to his office to do just that. He's probably so excited to have more work to do.

I catch Shadow's haunted eyes.

"Are you ok?"

He raises his eyebrows at me. "Yeah, she smells nice. I don't know about that male scent on her."

"It was odd, wasn't it?"

"This is happening quickly," he says to himself.

"Have you ever been with an omega in heat?" I ask, knowing the answer. None of us have.

He shakes his head. What have we gotten ourselves into?

"I like her hair," he whispers, and I smile. She does have nice hair. It's short and I can imagine my hands on her scalp, pulling her hair as she...

There are too many pheromones in the air. It's fucking with me.

She's quiet. Exactly how you want an omega to be. I wonder if I can get her to scream.

There I go again!

Shadow gives me a rare smile. "What're you thinking about?"

I return his smile. I think this strange little omega may actually help him. Is this the answer we've been waiting for? Omegas can do a lot for a pack. I am looking forward to watching her fix all of our problems.

4

Hot Hot Heat

Ondine

This is my nest. Just like the one at the Clinic. This is my nest, I repeat, trying to convince myself it's true. But I know, and the omega in me knows, this isn't one Arnie artfully prepared for me.

But I don't deserve that nice nest. I deserve this cold, spare bedroom. This cold bedroom in a strange house, miles out of the city, across a river, in a house with untrained, random alpha men, who apparently need an omega to help their sullen pack mate..

They think I can help? With what, my magic omega pussy? I shake my head and sigh. I put my bag on a dresser and look at myself in the mirror that is hung above it. I don't look as bad as I feel. My hair is a little out there, but it looks kind of cool. I fluff up the roots of my hair, the feeling helps calm me down.

Who the hell are these people, and why were they denied placement?

I am about to let them into my nest, so the answer to these questions better not be deal breakers. I have no choice. This is my only path forward.

Since I perfumed last spring, I've only been with strange alphas. At least with the Clinic, I knew they were safe and well trained.

Once I go into heat, I won't have much control. If my omega doesn't like them, she won't let them into the nest at all. I will be a slave to my instincts. At least none of them smelled bad to me. One of them smelled like oranges, and that was nice. A good orangey musk.

It's so depressing that one alpha's orange scent is the only thing I can hold on to right now.

But I can't feel bad for myself when Arnie is most likely ruined because of my omega. If I am being honest, I didn't even try to hold back when my instincts took over. I made that choice.

A tear escapes my eye, and I wipe it away.

At the first sign of emotion, my body lurches forward, and my stomach cramps. And it hurts! I yell out and fall to my knees. It's not another heat spike. This could be it. This could be my heat. It's fucking powerful.

I crawl to the bed and yank the quilt and sheets off. I pull it into an acceptable corner of the room where a thick, plush rug awaits me. Inside the closet, I find folded blankets and things I can use for my nest. Another cramp hits, and I cry out. Can they hear me?

I wish Arnie were here, getting an alpha ready to lead me through this like it's his job. Because it was.

I'm crying and panting. This hurts worse than ever. I need relief quickly. In the contract, it said that the alphas were required to help me through my heat. So I know they won't reject me, but a stupid primal fear peaks its ugly head, saying they won't want some girl with baggy clothes writhing on their floor. That's not pretty or sexy.

I arrange pillows around my nest, then manage to close the curtains. I like it when it's dark. I like pink and violet lighting too, but I won't get that here.

"Please," I cry as loud as I can manage. "Help."

Two sets of feet run up the stairs, then Sebastian and Shadow enter the room.

"Fuck, already?" Sebastian says.

"Please, I need someone."

"Can you smell that?" Shadow says.

"I think they could smell that on the moon. My dick is so hard. I'll go get Jake. You help her."

And with that, Sebastian is gone.

***

Shadow

It smells like sex incarnate here. Her pheromones permeate the air like a fog. I've never felt this before. She mewls in the middle of her nest, trying and failing to take off her shirt.

I steadily walk over to her, my anticipation growing.

This is new. This is different. I'm taking slow, deliberate breaths through my mouth, and I'm drooling.

I crouch down in front of her. "Ondine, what do you need?"

She tries again to take off her clothes. "Help."

I reach out with shaking hands and grab the hem of her tank top. I help her pull it over her head. Her breasts spill out of her small bralette. It offered no support. Her breasts come out from both the top and bottom of it. It makes me growl just looking at them. I need them in my mouth.

That's an odd thought.

I have to admit this whole thing is strange. I can't believe it's even working. I'm feeling more turned on and excited than I have in years.

She tugs down her pants, and I get them down her legs, along with her panties. In no time, this woman is completely naked in front of me.

And she's a goddamned vision.

It's like I've been asleep for years and am finally opening my eyes.

Every dip and turn of her body excites me.

This is weird. I've never once felt a sexual attraction to an omega, not like this. Where it feels important. Is this just my carnal self? Do all alphas feel this way with an omega in heat? Or is she special...she is a gift from my alpha.

Her scent grows even more than before as she moves to her hands and knees, presenting herself to me. I groan, and a purr starts up deep in my chest.

I place my cool hand on her heated skin. Her spine is covered in a layer of desperate sweat. I push her gently down so she's resting on her elbows. Then I glide my palms over her round ass. Just an hour ago, I was online arguing with someone on a forum defending an old, dead poet, and now here I am. A writhing, beautiful omega is presenting her ass to me like I'm some sort of prince.

She pushes back into my crotch, and my hard dick throbs in pain. I take off my belt and unzip myself from my pants.

I'm really doing this, aren't I? I'm really going to fuck this girl. The girl my alpha got for me. Brought home for me. He did this for me.

I use my finger to see how wet she is. Omegas produce their own slick everywhere back here. I could fuck her ass if I wanted to without getting any lube. But I am trying to be very gentle.

She's so wet, my fingers glide over her effortlessly. She moans into my touch, and I shudder.

I grab my dick and pass the tip up and down her slick.

"Yes, Alpha. Please, Alpha. I need you. It hurts," she cries.

How could I deny her after that?

I push my tip into her throbbing cunt. We both make horrendous sounds as I push into her. I'm not stopping. I'm not waiting for her to adjust. I'm just getting inside. And now. I can't wait. My ears are ringing, and the air is filled with lust and primal need.

The moment I bottom out, my knot not included, I fuck her. I fuck her like she's mine.

And she smells like mine.

She smells like a cold freezer full of vanilla ice cream. She smells like how my dreams smell.

She's screaming in pleasure but still begging for my knot. She won't find relief until I knot her.

I've knotted an omega only once before. But not while in heat. But my body knows what to do. It was designed for it.

Jake and Sebastian enter the room and take in the scene. They both smile at me as I rut into the back of her. Her ass is high, and her face pressed into the ground, her arms all the way on the rug in front of her.

"Fuck me, Shadow, you look happy," Jake marvels.

I pick up speed, and just when I think she can't take anymore, I push my knot into her. She screams and begs for more, with that sweet voice of hers, and Jake grabs his dick over his pants at the scene.

"Yes, Alpha, yes," she mutters into the pillows.

She's panting so hard I'm worried she'll pass out. Actually, she just may.

I rut into her a few more times before I come inside her.

She's completely passed out by the time I catch my breath. "Did you just kill her with your dick, Shadow?"

I roll my eyes. "She's asleep."

"Omegas pass out after being knotted when they are in heat," Sebastian clarifies.

"No shit? Well, good job then. I'll be back later. I'd like to fuck her in her mouth. Text me." And with that, Jake is gone.

I roll the two of us into a comfortable spot in the nest. She did a pretty job putting it together this quickly. I'm still inside her and will be for a while. Probably 30-40 minutes.

Sebastian takes a seat on a chair by the window.

"How did it feel?" he asks me quietly.

I nod. Still out of breath. "Exciting. She was begging for me. And now she's so content. It's a pretty great feeling."

He nods at me. Fascinated with the whole thing.

"Hey," he says apprehensively, "We never talked about what Boone said a few weeks ago. During poker."

I hold my breath. No, we have not. Boone, despite parading as our friend, revealed a secret I'd been harboring for years. Maybe he was drunk, and that's why it came out, but fuck him anyway. Boone and I have never been close, so I don't even know when he got this out of me. Maybe it was just a good guess.

"Was he correct?"

Was he correct? That I'd been holding a flame for my alpha for years? Absolutely spot on. Like he'd known the true intent of my heart.

But he's probably not asking about Jake. Of course not. He's asking about himself, and the little flame I carried for him as well.

I sigh. "Maybe I've had the wrong expectations of a pack. I know I'm too needy. I know I have a lot of issues. I've been trying to manage them."

Sabbies shakes his head. "Why didn't you ever say anything?"

"Because it's embarrassing. Jake and I were incredible for like two weeks. And then he was done. He'd done what he always does, made me fall for him, and that was it for him. And with you, Sabbies. Come on, I sit with you during pack parties. You judge everyone for what they do and do not do. If not everyone in a pack has a bond mark, then they are just asking to be broken. If they are all male pack with a male omega, you make rude comments about babies. If they have too many female alphas. Or two omegas. You wouldn't accept what I wanted. You think you'd let our pack, that's not even fully formed with no omega, start intimate relationships? You would have been horrified by the offer if I repeated it."

He bows his head and puts his hands over his face. "Am I that bad?"

"Yes."

"I'm sorry."

"This is a weird conversation to have while my dick is inside of someone," I mutter.

"Yeah," he confirms.

I lay my head down and rest. Eventually, my knot relaxes and I slip out of her. I go to get Jake. She'll be awake soon.

5

Office Pet

Ondine

My heat lasts just a day and a half. I'm barely conscious, but I hardly have to beg for it. One of the three of them was more than happy to step in. Jake made me drink water. Sebastian got me more nesting materials. Shadow was usually the one actually knotting me. Jake just wanted to fuck my face (something I definitely needed to satiate my intense heat).

When I'm finally no longer 110 degrees and horny as a freight train, I'm starting to get a clear picture of what kind of mess I'm in.

As I wash my face in the sink, I can't help but think about how no one will wonder where I am. Every time my heat cools off, I feel a not insignificant amount of feelings.

And today, I feel alone.

Loneliness is something I wear every day, but some days I actually feel it on me.

The Meier pack, while inexperienced, didn't let me down entirely. It is, after all, just fucking. And I don't ask for the other stuff. The petting. The sweet talk. The cuddling. The kissing.

The omega in me wants that, but she's used to being deprived.

I get my first proper meal from Emmerson in the kitchen. He's the beta I first sort of met when I got here. Emil is their groundskeeper. Ellie is their housekeeper. No, I'm not making that up. No one has an explanation for me.

Emmerson makes me eggs piled on sourdough bread with strawberries and mangoes on the side. I've eaten two whole plates. He's smiling at me, but I'm hesitant to return the smile.

Jake comes in to get a protein shake. He's sweaty from a run. He seems surprised to see me, stopping short at my presence, then he checks out my outfit and is pleased, giving me a wry smile.

"How're you feeling this morning?" he asks. But I don't answer right away, so he moves on. "You look well enough. Come into my office later. Let's say, 11:30. Wear something cute."

And then he leaves.

Wear something cute? I borrowed these shorts, which are really men's boxers, from the laundry. I look at Emmerson, who is trying to pretend he wasn't listening.

"What does he mean by wearing something cute? I don't have anything."

He puts up his hands in defeat. He's older. Unlike Jake. Who, I think, is the youngest alpha in the pack. Emmerson is probably in his late forties. Like a *rough* late 40s.

I need to get some things to wear. For the last couple days, I've been naked, so it's been a non-issue. I hop off the stool and look around the house for Sebastian or Shadow. I find Sebastian out back with Emil, digging up pavers and putting them into a wheelbarrow.

"Hello, Alpha. Can you drive me to the department store? I need some clothes and things."

He stretches up tall, wiping sweat from his brow, puts his hands on his hips, and then finally looks at me. I'm standing on the porch, as patient and pertinent as possible.

"Did you check your room? I left clothes and things on your bed earlier."

I don't really know what to think of that. Did he buy me clothes? Or did he just find some things? Unable to form a question, I thank him and go to my room. My bed is made, and there are some stacks of brand new clothes, three boxes of shoes, socks, and panties. Lying out next to the stacks are a few sundresses. Men love sundresses. There are no bras.

Did Sebastian pick out all of this? The style is so specific. Boho, floral, with pinks and whites. I take some things to the bathroom across the hall. There are new things on the countertop for me. Makeup. Shampoo. Combs and brushes. Face wash. I get myself together. I wear a sundress to Jake's office.

I go barefoot since I'm just in the house.

I have no clue what to expect, and I shouldn't expect anything, anyway. I'm hardly aware how I even got here to begin with.

It feels like everything from that first heat spike to now has been a fever dream.

I knock and then let myself in. Jake stands behind a wooden desk, looking out the window while on the phone. He turns to wave me over to him. I shut the door and walk closer to the desk. He impatiently gestures for me to join him on his side.

He's still on the phone.

"Yes, Freddie, I understand. But nothing has happened yet. I've called Senator Wong's office already. His people are taking the threat seriously. What would you have me do?" He's talking in a very professional tone, but the way he's fucking me with his eyes is telling a whole different story.

He directs my body so I'm facing the desk and the door. His hands grab my hips and pull me into his, right over his hard-on. Oh. That's why I'm here.

Jake apparently has one use for me.

He leans down and whispers, "Be quiet, little omega, and I'll reward you. I like this dress on you."

He slides the thin straps off my shoulders and then exposes my chest. He fondles my breasts and pulls my nipples until I'm panting and needy. God, I spent days in an absolute spell of lust and arousal, and here I am again.

Jake continues talking over the phone, "I'll make sure I have more than that ready. You know me, Freddie, I won't let you down."

Since I've been an omega, I haven't had sex outside of my heat or spikes. This is new.

He pushes me down until my upper body is totally on his desk, my arms out wide. I have to push his laptop out of the way.

He pulls my dress up until it's all piled around my waist, and then he rubs my ass and hips.

"Right, right, but you can't just ask for something like that and expect me not to provide you with new pricing. I'll give you double the security and resources, but expect double the price. You're family, but this is still our business. I should honestly charge you more because you are family."

Jake unbuckles his belt and opens up his slacks.

He's going to fuck me right here.

Just as I think that, he pushes his dick into me. Because I am already wet for him, it only takes a few tight thrusts for most of him to get inside. He shows me how he wants me to rock back into him, and so I do. I let out a moan, and he slaps his hand over my mouth. I get some good leverage on the desk with my arms and then push back into him over and over while he talks to someone about god knows what. He's not quite inside me yet, but damn, it feels good.

"I understand. But our intel is good. Your father is in danger. Whether it warrants your involvement or not—"

There's a knock at the door, and Sebastian walks in, alarmed to see us in this position. Jake waves him in.

"Ok, sounds good. We've got a plan, Alpha Wong. I'll get you that new quote by the end of the day, and I'll look out for your signature. Take care—"

Jake gets off the phone, then takes over the fucking.

"Hey, Sabbies, what do you need?" He says almost casually, almost because he grunts right at the end.

"I was going to offer to have lunch together, but it seems you're busy."

"Join us. I bet she'd like both her holes filled," Jake says, and it doesn't sound like a suggestion. Sebastian definitely doesn't take it as one. He moves the chair and comes up to the other side of the desk, where my face is. He puts his hand on my cheek like he's assessing how to best go about this.

I don't even feel like I'm in the room with them. But my body betrays me because I am flushed and wanting.

"Has she sucked your dick yet?" Jake asks.

"Yeah, and it was heaven," he croaks out. Then he pulls down the front of his pants, and before I know it, he opens my mouth with his hand. "Tongue out, sweetheart."

I open my mouth and lay my tongue out. He presses his dick far into my mouth, and I swallow it so it goes down into my throat. He nearly falls to his knees.

"Good fuck, she's good at that."

"Fuck her mouth, Sabbies. I want to see it."

They both work me from either end until they get a pleasant rhythm, and I'm able to let go. I let them do what they want.

I let my mind detach from my body as they fuck me together. Is it bad that being used like this feels slightly freeing? I would never admit that being treated like a hole is helping me feel less lonely. But damn, it's easy to just *be* when I'm like this.

Jake tells Sebastian to come in me, but tells me not to swallow because he wants to see. He puts a bit of alpha voice in his command, so it's easy for me to just comply.

He pulls out of me and stands me up, spinning me to face him. "Show me," he commands. I open my mouth and show him Sebastian's cum. He growls and then sits down on his armless chair, bringing me with him. I straddle his waist, and he's already inside me. His mouth on my nipple. I fuck him until he cums. He is not quick, and by the end, I am a sweaty, desperate thing.

I don't rest on his chest, but I'd so love to. It seems so nice. But I know better. Jake isn't one for sensuality or intimacy. He's proven that during my Heat. This is just fucking. And he's barely even asked me what I want. I'm being nice. He hasn't asked at all. I turn and look at Sebastian, who has the decency to look a bit guilty.

"Ok, baby, off you go. Sabbies and I are about to have lunch."

I do as he says without hesitation. It was barely an hour and I get my day back.

As I am about to leave the door, he says, "You better seek out Shadow before the end of the day and give him what he needs."

I tell him I will, happy to have guidance on what exactly he wants from me while I'm here.

***

Ondine

Later that night, I knock on Shadow's bedroom door, but he doesn't answer it. Eventually, I decide to just open it. His familiar old-world fruity smell greets me. His room is cluttered, but well designed. He's got shelving on all the walls, filled with books. Stacks of books but up against couches and chairs and all around his bed. His windows are covered with jewel tone velvet fabrics. There are all these little orange glow lamps everywhere that remind me of fireflies.

Shadow is on a wingback chair with a little pink book in his lap. He's looking at me, but not. Maybe he is high or something. I take in a deep breath, hoping to smell some weed, but all I smell are figs and honey.

"Jake asked me to spend the evening with you," I say. He's an alpha and I'm an omega. This should be easy enough. It's after dinner time, we'd all eaten separately, but there was soup and rolls on the kitchen counter that I ate quite a bit of.

"What do omegas do in the evenings with a pack?" He asks.

I shrug.

He doesn't ask me again, so I shut the door behind me and walk into his space. There's a loveseat across from him, and I sit down in it. There are some open books I have to move out of the way.

"What do you want to do?" I ask.

He sighs and puts his book in his pocket.

Will he want me to fuck him like Jake and Sabbies? I don't think I'd mind. Yesterday, he gripped my hips in a way that felt so possessive and delicious. I observe his hands now. He has long fingers. Good hands.

"What did you do for Jake?"

I smile a little and tell him all about it.

But he doesn't let a single detail go.

"What did he say exactly?" "What did he feel like going in?" "Did he moan or groan?" "Did he kiss you? Where?" and they don't stop. He makes me go over it again and again.

I lay back on the love seat, annoyed at how many times I have to talk about it. Eventually, he stops, but then simply excuses me for the night. Confused and dejected, I leave him alone.

And so goes my days at the Meier pack. I eat breakfast. Get ready. Fuck Jake in his office. Sometimes he wants me to lay my head in his lap while he works and then suck him off. Other times, he wants me to rock slowly in his lap while he works. Mostly, he likes to bend me over and fuck me. Sebastian comes in and joins nearly every day. We do this every day but Friday.

And in the evenings after dinner, I find Shadow, and he makes me recall every detail of my time with Jake and then sends me to bed.

No cuddling. No spooning. No hugging. No kissing.

It's so fucking awful.

No wonder the Institute wasn't going to let them have an omega.

6

From the Shadows

Ondine

F our days after I left the train station with Jake, a police officer
came to the house. Jake must have known he was on his way, because he's ready for him when he arrives. They talk in the entryway for
a while, and I listen in from the piano room. Their low, professional,
and friendly murmuring can be easily heard from the other room.

"I just have to check for my records, and we can all move on."

"I understand," Jake replies.

"With all the missing omegas lately, people get spooked, you
know?"

"How many are missing?"

"That's the thing, none. Two had been reported missing by their
handlers or family, but all have been located and are safe."

"Really? They're safe? So, was it a coincidence?"

"No, not a coincidence. They'd all been taken, that's true. And
you didn't hear it from me, Alpha Meier, but they were all taken by
someone affiliated with the same...local businessman."

"Is it who I think it is?"

"Yeah."

There's silence.

"But the omegas are safe?"

"Safe and accounted for. Your omega was reported missing days ago, and we assumed she was taken in the same manner. Good thing we reached out to you. You say she's been here?"

"Temporary placement. I sent a copy of the contract for your records."

"Perfect. I just need to speak with her. You're welcome to stay."

Jake leads the officer into the piano room. I'm sitting on a window seat, with my phone out, like I'd been watching a video. The uniformed officer bends his head to me.

"Hello, I'm Officer Sanchez. I just need to ask you some questions, is that alright?"

I nod my head. Jake sits at the piano, legs out wide, watching the officer carefully.

"What is your name and designation?"

"Ondine. Omega."

"And are you here on your own free will?"

"Yes. Who reported me missing?"

"The Heat Clinic that you were scheduled to be at last week. You never arrived."

So, was it Arnie who reported me, or the Clinic itself? Arnie knew I had been there. Did he just let me go? Didn't try to find me? Didn't report me missing?

"Did you need to speak to me in private about any matter?" The officer asks, and I shake my head no. He's satisfied with the constraints of his report. He says thank you and leaves the house, escorted by Jake.

Jake comes back into the room and stares at me for a minute. I stare back. I want to ask him about the missing omegas, but he just found out as I did. I'm glad they're safe, but it makes me wonder what happened to them. He eventually leaves me alone with my thoughts.

***

Shadow

Ondine plays the piano as I watch from the entryway. Does she know she looks like a whole different woman when she plays?

It's like she turns on a light in a dark room, illuminating herself as *Ondine*. A girl we shouldn't underestimate. Talented people often invoke this awe in others. Like we are walking among gods. Or goddesses. I could write poetry about her. Her bare feet on the pedals. Her dextrous fingers over the keys with her clipped fingernails.

God, she's so pretty.

She has a bow in her hair.

Jake is in his office. He usually has her come to him around 11:00 am. But it won't happen today. It's been two weeks since we've had her here. Two weeks is Jake's threshold for relationships. He's going to start pulling back on her.

I've been so upset watching him lead her along. He's been feeding her. Giving her gifts, like a tv, and more and more clothes. He's also had her in his office every day (but Friday) fucking her, having her sit pretty on a chair, or sitting between his legs on the floor with her head in his lap. I haven't seen it, but I've been asking her to tell me about it.

It's going to hurt her when he pulls back. When he loses interest. He should have been careful.

It hurt me when he pulled back. There's still a piece of my heart beating outside of my chest that he unknowingly carries with him.

I can't sit around and watch him do it to someone else.

Ondine is temporary, and he shouldn't be treating her like this.

She finishes her song and checks the time on her phone. I pull back to hide further into the shadows, so she doesn't know I'm here.

She straightens her skirt and the bow in her hair and then heads off into the house towards Jake's office.

I'm right behind her. She doesn't know.

She stands at the office door for a breath. What is she thinking? Why does she pause?

She opens the door, and I settle myself to listen through a thin spot in the wall.

I hear Jake exclaim, "Baby!"

But I can't distinguish much else. It's highly likely I won't hear anything at all until Ondine tells me about it tonight. I'll have to listen to her disappointed tale of how Jake won't touch her anymore.

Then she and I will lean on each other until her contract runs out. From a distance. At arm's length.

I haven't even touched her since her heat, and she's already burrowing herself into me. Any new piece of information I learn only further proves she'd make a great omega for this pack.

But she's temporary.

She wants to go home.

We shouldn't have done this.

Suddenly, I hear moaning. The omega is moaning. Are they fucking?

I press my ear to the wall.

Somehow, this is worse.

This doesn't make me feel good at all. If she and Jake keep going down this road, it'll be even worse when she leaves. I can't do a month of this.

I keep listening as she comes not once, but twice.

My feet carry me right through his office door. Ondine is sitting in his office chair while he's on his knees, face in her pussy, eating her out. I look up at the wall with the windows overlooking the river. The sounds coming from them beckon me. The smells in this office—her cold vanilla ice cream smell and his birthday cake smell. It's everything in me to resist its beck and call.

Jake pulls down Ondine's top, revealing her perfect tits and their little pink nipples.

"Jake," I confidently say. He doesn't stop. And I can see why. She's close. He pulls at one of her nipples, and it nearly sends her over the edge.

"Jake?" I say louder.

Don't look at her. If she looks me in the eyes when she's like this...

He doubles his efforts. I have to stand here helpless as he goes after her clit like it's the only thing in this world and the next.

Finally, Ondine comes.

And it's so pretty.

She's so pretty.

It's absolutely devastating.

Jake smiles up at her. Calls her a good omega. And then stands and faces me, with the most proud look on his face.

"My dear Shadow, have you come at last to join us?" I suck in a breath. How would it be to be able to join them? God.

"Can I talk to you?" I glance at Ondine as she gets her feet under her and adjusts her clothes. "Alone?"

He places his hands on his hips and turns to Ondine. He sighs at her as she decides not to put her panties back on, but just holds them in her hand.

"Sure. Yeah," he says to me, and then to Ondine, "I'll come find you again soon, little omega. Don't go far."

He kisses her on the forehead and takes her panties from her. Pocketing them.

"Ok," she says, then passes by me on her way out. I don't breathe the whole time. I don't want to risk smelling her even more.

"What's going on?" Jake adjusts his dick in his pants. He made her come three times and didn't even take his dick out. Good god.

"I don't think this is working. Having her here."

"What do you mean?"

"Your behavior..."

"What about it?"

"You're acting obsessed, Jake," I meet his eyes. "Crazed. Possessive. Is it going to suddenly stop?" *Like it did with me.* "Or is it not going to end, and then she leaves us, and you won't let her go? Either way, I'm worried."

He doesn't move. It's like I've caught him. Finally, he says, "I like her."

"No shit. But don't you see this can only end badly?"

He turns to the window to look out over the river. He's chewing on my words.

"Shadow," he says, in a tone so loving it makes me weepy in spite of myself. "She's just here for the contract. A good fuck. To help balance our hormones."

Bullshit, I think, because we can't keep her. This was supposed to be temporary. Does he even hear himself?

I can't spend my days while she's here, creeping around every corner, watching her. And Jake is practically doing the same thing. He checks in on her at night. I know because I'm fucking watching him, too.

I wipe my hand down my face. "No, something else is happening here. I've never seen you act like this with anyone."

He sighs and waves me over to him so we can both look out the window.

"Nothing is happening. Why don't you give her a chance to be what you need her to be? That's a command. We have four weeks left until her next heat. Don't waste it being worried."

Then Jake does something he knows I love. He puts his hand on the side of my neck and bends my head down in a small submissive pose, then he mirrors it, pushing our foreheads together. It's a gesture I've only seen alphas do with each other during mating ceremonies. Except he's Jake, so he continues to force my head down a little lower than his. It makes me laugh, and I resist him until he gives up. But he'll try again.

"It's going to be ok," he says. And I try to believe him.

7

To the Salon!

Ondine

J ake is not letting up. I fear he's getting obsessed. He's never once referred to me by name. He's never asked a single question about me. But he has suddenly become very interested in how many orgasms I have every day, if I'm eating enough, if I have everything I need for a bubble bath, and now there are stacks of new sheet music on my bed.

I'm afraid I don't know what to do with this kind of attention.

It's Tuesday when I'm sitting between his legs, head on his thigh, while he works. He's taken to stroking my hair and neck. Playing with my earlobe. I can't help the purr that comes out of me. Omegas are such suckers for being touched. He keeps touching me in ways that continue to make me purr. I finally have to stop him.

"Alpha Meier," I say with my stupidly soft voice.

"Yes, baby?" he replies halfway, listening. I can feel the rumble of his voice on his thigh.

"I have a hair appointment this afternoon. Can I take a car into the city?"

He pauses and then types out a message to someone on his computer.

"You don't like it much longer than this?" he asks, tugging my hair. It surprises me since he never asks me a question about myself like this.

"I don't like the feel of it on my neck."

"Can it wait until Friday?" he asks, eventually.

I can't really form an answer. "No? My appointment is today. Why Friday?"

"I go into the city on Fridays to visit my mom. I could take you with me."

A sudden realization that Jake is human and has human parents hits me.

"Make your next appointment on a Friday," he says. "My mother is in a care facility in the Riverfront District, so if it is nearby, that would be even easier."

Jake visits his mother in a care facility every Friday. That's where he's been these last two times. I am also hung up on the fact that Jake thinks I will still be around the next time I need a haircut. And did he just imply that I would see his mother during this time, too?

Sebastian enters his office as I am trying to decide how to tell him I won't have another cut until after my next heat.

"What's up, Jake?"

He looks at me on the floor and smiles.

"Ondine has a hair appointment in the city this afternoon. Can you take her?"

Sebastian shrugs his shoulders. "Boone and I were going to go shooting, but we can take the little omega into the city instead." He seems excited.

"What neighborhood, baby?"

"Kestrel Burrow," I reply.

He stops stroking my hair.

"Where I saw you crying and reeking of some male?" He pushes his chair back and away from me. I stand up and move away. Looking at both alphas.

"Yes, that's my neighborhood. Where my apartment is."

The mood has shifted

"Where your apartment is?"

"Yeah, did you think I fell out of the sky? Fully formed?"

"Maybe," he whispers. "Who's watching your apartment now?"

"No one." I had it cleaned up for my heat. I was planning on being at the Heat Clinic for four or five days. It's been a few weeks, but it's fine there until I go back. My landlady keeps the area pretty secure. She'd call me if there were issues, I think.

Jake does something odd. He growls. I notice he has fisted his hands. His jaw is tight. Why is this a problem?

"Is everything ok, Alpha?" I ask slowly.

Then I look at Sebastian, who looks worried as well as upset.

"No, I'm fine. You'll go to your hair appointment and come right back to me? And listen to Sebastian? He's there to make sure you're safe."

I nod. "Yes."

He relaxes, but only slightly. "Does that man, the one who had you, does he live in that neighborhood?"

He means Arnie. *The man that had me* is such a weird way to refer to Arnie. Did he have me?

But Jake is acting possessive. Is this part of the fun of a temporary placement? Pretending like you are bonded? Is that what's happening?

"I don't know."

"How do you know him?"

"I'd rather not say. You're scaring me."

He growls, but it seems like it's mostly at himself. My hands are sweaty, and I wipe them on my skirt.

"Fine. Sabbies, don't let her out of your sight. Bring her right back here. You understand?"

He smiles like he knows a secret. "Yes, Alpha," he answers a bit sarcastically.

Jake turns to me, "Ok, well, don't cut your hair too short. I'll see you this evening."

I don't know why, but that comment suddenly makes me come unglued. "I'll cut my hair however short I want," I bite at him.

He's taken aback by my tone, and his eyes are wide like discs. "Excuse me?"

Sebastian jumps in, "Jake, you don't tell women what to do with their hair. You know that."

Jake grumbles something indiscernible. "Yes, of course." He turns and gives me a fake smile. "Do you need money for the service?"

He's only offering because he messed up.

"Yes, please." I have no shame.

He opens a drawer and pulls out an envelope with some cash. "How much?"

I don't know why this number pops into my head, but I say it anyway, "Five hundred dollars."

Jake only hesitates for a moment before pulling out five one-hundred-dollar bills and passing them to me. As soon as they are in my hand, I say thank you and dart out of the room.

***

Sebastian

I turn to Jake, who looks a bit lost.

He asks, "A haircut doesn't cost five hundred dollars, does it?"

I try my best not to laugh. "No."

He grumbles some of his favorite swear words and then goes back to his desk. "I handle her better if we aren't talking."

"I don't know. I think she's just as thrilling when she has something to say."

It's really entertaining to see Jake meet his match. He waves his hand, dismissing me and this idea. "Boone will be with you?"

"Yeah, is that a problem, Alpha?"

"No, I have no issues with Boone. If he wasn't available, I would have asked you to take a team. You'll be good with just the two of you?"

"You're doubting my ability to keep the omega safe?"

Jake sighs dramatically. "Of course not."

I heard about the missing omegas as well. Both were unbonded. Taken in plain sight as the sun was shining. I called my contacts with the police to get the rest of the story. They'd been taken and then both bonded to different alphas. One with a pack, and one with a single alpha. My contact assured me they're fine.

Jake is clearly worried about her.

But I have to address the larger matter:

"Shadow isn't getting any better," I say to my pack lead. "Our bond is still heavy. He's spending less time out of the house. More time alone. He's not finishing his meals."

Jake acts like he isn't listening to me at first. He's moving things around his office, cleaning up from the day.

"Jake?"

He sighs. "I know. He just needs to…" He can't finish his sentence. We don't know what to do.

"What are we going to do?" I ask anyway. Maybe rhetorically.

He looks at me this time. He doesn't know. When has Jake ever not known what to do?

I leave him alone in his office and go to find the little omega. Shadow may not be getting better, but she sure is establishing herself. It's been weeks, and I've never seen her act that way around him. Hell, she's never once talked about her life outside of here. I'm with Jake. I started to believe she fell out of the sky and was at our mercy.

But that's largely to do with the fact I've been avoiding being alone with her. She's here for Shadow, and I don't want to get in the way of that. Doesn't mean I don't want to be around her. She's like this pretty little fairy creature flitting through the house. Appearing in rooms suddenly. Smelling like a vanilla ice cream sundae. The only time I indulge is when Jake asks me to join them. I'd love to crawl into her room at night, lie at her feet…kiss her knees. But she's not here for me. She's here for Shadow. And in a month, she will be gone.

I know he said to go there and back, but we are totally going to this apartment. I want to see if this place smells like vanilla ice cream—Ondine's sweet scent.

I find her in the music room at the piano, playing a soft melody. She's got a floral skirt and a tank top on. It's so spectacular having a girly girl in the house. The other day, she wore a headband with a bow. I think she looks good. I think she looks like we go together. I've got my blue jeans and a white shirt. Maybe she'd like earrings to match my one.

I grab her, and we head out. We pick up Boone at his office. He's a lawyer when he's not a renegade. He's got his cowboy hat and boots on. We look like a bunch of hicks, honestly.

His smile is from ear to ear when he sees Ondine in the cab of my truck.

"Well, we ain't going shooting, are we?"

"No, we got a little mission. We're taking this little omega to her hair appointment in the city."

Boone zeroes in on her, and she responds by squirming in her seat.

As we are driving over the bridge to the city, held up by some traffic, she leans over and asks quietly, "Boone is an alpha? Is he in your pack?"

It is a bit odd to be friends with a stray alpha. It's one of those exceptions I have for my affiliations. Boone is a good alpha. And we met when he was looking for a pack. Jake's parents know his parents, and they grew up near each other. Boone on a ranch and Jake in the suburban neighborhood nearby.

He's been my friend for a while, despite the fact that Boone and Shadow don't get along.

"He's an alpha. Unattached. Unbonded. He's vetting out packs. We offered him a spot, but he declined us. Wants to keep his options open."

She glances quickly behind her to the smiling Boone. "Yes, maybe you should contract with me next, sweet omega. What do you say?"

I drop my smile when I see a blush creep up her face. "Stop that, Boone. That's really inappropriate behavior."

"Why? Isn't this a temporary placement? Or did something change?"

I don't answer him. Nothing has changed. She's gone in a month. Or whenever her next heat is. She's just a nice smelling omega, so my alpha brain gets confused.

And there's no way we can keep her if she's not helping Shadow.

8

Blush

Sebastian

Ondine directs me to a good parking spot, in between the salon and her place. I shot a quick text to Jake about stopping over. I can't lie to him. He responds quickly, agreeing it's a good idea to check it out.

Boone is already leading Ondine by the small of her back into the salon. That fresh motherfucker. I jog over to meet them inside. The place is small and older. Two giant alphas take up all the waiting area space. Boone manages not to knock over anything. I'm not so lucky.

"Ondine! Oh my god, look at you! I've never seen you in a skirt!" A woman with long, beautiful, brown hair wearing all black greets my girl at the counter. Not my girl. Just Ondine. They hug and compliment each other a few more times.

"And who are these men? Are they yours?"

Her face goes pink again, and I'm jealous for the second time that it's not me who's made her blush like that.

"Sort of. This is Sebastian. He's with the pack I'm in placement with right now. Just temporary." It's everything in me not to growl. I really don't like how everyone keeps bringing up—it's only temporary. "And this is Boone. He's...Boone?"

Boone tips his hat at the stylist, and she blushes, too. This is ridiculous.

"Well, it's nice to see you with alphas. It's about time you spend time with one outside of the Clinic."

She doesn't respond and looks a bit sheepish. The stylist and her leave us to go to the chair to start her appointment. I overhear her say, "I'm guessing it didn't work out with that beta. Did you tell him how you feel?"

Ondine whips her head to me, her eyes the size of moons. She knows I overheard. And it's something she didn't want me to hear.

Next to me, Boone says, "A beta?"

"Don't be rude, Boone. They aren't talking to us."

But I'm just as curious as he is.

I hear her friend say sorry and change the subject.

Was it a beta that caused her to run into the train station, crying, hours away from a heat? He wouldn't have been able to help her, anyway. An omega needs an alpha during heat. She needs a knot. A beta would just frustrate her. It would cause pain and suffering. Is that why she needed a Heat Clinic, because she'd been dating a beta? How very odd.

Boone rummages around for a few more minutes before barreling into the salon and sitting in a chair next to the women. He asks both of them a million questions. Stupid questions.

"What are you looking forward to most?"

"How would you feel if your plans were canceled?"

"When no one is around, what do you cook for yourself?"

I'm getting tired of it. I guess Ondine is looking forward to the full moon. She likes to see it every time it comes around. She expects plans to get canceled. And she cooks herself shrimp tacos when she's alone. She's always alone, she says.

The cut is done. It looks like it did before, just shinier. And her neck looks longer. I tell her this. But she doesn't blush.

Hm. I'll try again.

"I'm hungry. Let's get something to eat!" Boone declares on the street.

"No, we don't have time. Jake wants us home for dinner, and I want to see Ondine's apartment."

He boos me. Ondine wasn't expecting the detour, but I say we will just check in on it. She can grab things she may need, too. She agrees, and we walk the two blocks to her street. Her apartment is on the basement level with its own walk out. As we descend the stairs, I turn to Boone.

"*Stay here.*" I don't mean to bark, but I do. He's shocked by my tone, but doesn't resist. I turn back and rush after Ondine.

She gets a spare key from the landlady, who's more than happy to let her in. I'm sure Ondine is a great tenant. She's always so quiet at the pack house—doesn't take more than she should and makes do.

It's a nice place. Not fancy, but it's a private room well decorated. Good furniture. As I stand near a velvet soft pink couch next to her bookshelf, surrounded by her things, I realize I don't know anything about her. I've fucked this woman into a coma more than once, but I don't know anything at all.

There's a keyboard prominently displayed. Stacks of sheet music and piano books littered around it. Pencils scattered underfoot. It's the only place that's messy in the entire apartment.

She waters some plants and looks through her cabinets. Then, bags up some trash. Near the bookshelf, there's a big purple beanbag chair, and I can't help but sink into it.

"This is a nice place," I remark.

"Thanks."

"How long have you been here?"

"Well, I moved in when I graduated college. So, a year?"

I'm watching her move about the place, taking care of little things. She starts gathering some clothes and shoes. I'm resisting the urge to help her. Plus, the beanbag chair is losing structure, and I am sinking further into it.

"What do you do?"

She stops and pushes her hair out of her face so she can get a good look at me. She's probably realizing she knows the taste of my cum, and yet I don't know where she works.

I don't want to resist this feeling.

"I'm a pianist. So I do lots of things. I'm a music teacher privately and at the charter high school downtown. I play piano for the ballet company during their practices. I take some gigs at a recording studio too. Some nights I play at a piano bar."

Her shelves next to me are flushed with music theory books and piano books.

"That's impressive. I don't know any omegas who are so talented and...independent."

She stops what she's doing and smiles at me. She's too far away to see if she's blushing. I've now sunk into this beanbag so far that there's no way I can get out of it without flailing about like a drunk starfish.

"Thank you. I'm not a great omega. I was certainly a good beta. I had lots of friends. A boyfriend. A job at the dance department. I was so excited to get my career started and get my own place. I wanted to be single and date, and live that city life. I am lucky. I have a trust fund from my parents. It's not much, but it covers my rent. Thank god. There's no way a musician could afford her own place like this. It's still not great, but I like this neighborhood. It's older, but friendly."

"What happened to the boyfriend?" I know I should ask better questions.

"We broke up right after graduation. He said I was *too agreeable*. Joke's on him—it was the omega in me."

I laugh. I can't help it. "Ondine, I have three sisters who are omegas. Agreeableness is not an omega trait. I can assure you."

"Three!"

"And two alpha brothers. I come from a big pack. My omega mom was big on babies."

"Wow," she says and then zips up a bag.

"What about you?"

"What about me?"

"What's your family like? Were they a big pack?"

She goes to the door. "You don't have to do this, Sebastian. It's fine. Ok? Let's just enjoy this, whatever it is, and not worry about it too much."

I have to get out of this beanbag chair.

"What're you talking about?"

"You don't have to ask me about my career or my family. We aren't dating. Your pack isn't courting me. Jake told me that Shadow was needing some companionship, and that's why you had a contract available. If you ask me, I think it's actually Jake who needs the companionship. But no matter. Let's go back to your house, and you can do what you want with me."

I don't like that. That doesn't feel right. The wrongness of it unsettles my entire body. I make the journey out of the beanbag chair. It's as awkward and painful as one could imagine.

Once I'm standing, I regain all my pride because she's just standing there, too. Bag in hand. Serene look on her face like nothing is wrong at all.

Does she not feel the wrongness?

I want to throttle her. Which is the thought I have as I eat up the space between us. I back her into the door, then gently remove the bag from her hands and set it on the ground next to us. Then I stand up tall, showing her how much taller I am than her.

"You won't get to know me?"

"I didn't say that."

"Yes, you did. You like Jake, you spend every evening with Shadow, but you don't like me?"

"Jake barely talks to me. Shadow doesn't look me in the eye and hasn't touched me since my heat."

Her confession rams through me like a deluge. I'd been giving her space to be with Shadow, so it didn't occur to me that he wasn't being good to her.

"Why didn't you..." I stop asking my question before I foolishly ask why she didn't come to me. She doesn't know she can come to me.

Jake doesn't talk to her, and Shadow doesn't look her in the eye or even touch her. I thought he liked her. Is he pushing her away? Things were fine after her heat. At least I thought so.

Have I been so blind?

"You can come to me. Talk to me."

She doesn't respond. It's all becoming so clear. Jake treats her like a pet, and I guess Shadow is withholding affection entirely. Her pretty, milky hazel eyes look up at me. She's always looking up at me. I don't mean to, but I have my hand in her hair. My other hand is on her waist. I want inside of her. I want to lift up her skirt and be inside of her here and now. The desire is almost overwhelming.

I've been holding back on coming to her because I wanted to give Shadow time to be with her. With our eyes locked, I decide I'm not going to do that anymore.

I'm not gonna hold back.

She realizes my breathing has changed, and I must have a wild look in my eyes because she makes a little gasp, and the sound goes right to my dick.

"Why did you leave Boone out there?" she asks in her soft voice. It's not an omega voice. That's not a thing. It's just her. Soft and quiet and agreeable.

"Because I wanted you all to myself. He was being greedy with you." I didn't realize how much that would affect this little omega. I was just being honest. But my words make her entire body shiver, and her knees wobble. I grab her before she falls, holding her up with my body, and she whistles a little noise from her chest.

"Whoa, there," I steady her.

Under her breath, she says, "When you act possessive, your scent changes."

"What?"

"Yeah, you usually smell the subtle scent of an orange. But just then, you smelled like those dried oranges—you know the ones they have in Old Fashions? You smelled like an Old Fashion with a dried orange. I didn't know that could happen." She won't meet my eyes. My hands are on her arms, still holding her steady, but she may not need it anymore. It may be me who needs it.

I've never…

I shake my head. I don't know what's happening.

I need to talk to my pack. This ends now. We need to talk to Shadow about how he's treating her. And if she isn't right for us, we have to end it now, before I become too interested.

I've always had a thing for musicians. And blondes.

"Come on, little omega. Let me get you home and fed." I take a risk and kiss her forehead before pulling away.

I may be just seeing things, but I think her cheeks pink a little.

I take her bag from her. We turn off the lights and finally leave. She locks up and drops off the key with the landlady, who has been chatting this whole time with Boone.

Oh, God. I can't take him anywhere. They act like best friends. Exchanging links to recipes and he sends her off with a reminder of the advice he had already bestowed upon her.

"Made another friend?" I tease Boone as we walk to the car. Ondine is keeping a noticeable distance from me.

"You left me alone with a stranger for thirty minutes while you banged your omega. What was I supposed to do?"

I hit him hard on the arm. "We didn't bang. We just needed a minute without you asking if she liked a bedroom that had morning or evening light more. Or whatever the hell you'd been asking at the salon."

"Oh, sorry, I didn't realize asking questions was going to upset you."

"That's a dumb thing to say."

Boone laughs at me. We get to the truck, and Ondine sits up front again. Thank god. I am not in the mood for more Boone.

I desperately want to be comfortable enough with her to put my hand on her leg. Or for her to rest her head on my arm instead of the window. Soon, I think, soon I'll be closer to her. After I show her how an alpha is supposed to care for an omega.

9

The Turn

Jake

Where the ever living fuck are Sabbies and Ondine? They left six hours ago. And for six miserable fucking hours, I've been unable to get a goddamned thing done. I've changed my clothes three times. Granted, I tried to go for a run. Opted instead for a cold shower. Then I was cold, so I took a hot shower.

Another omega was lifted off the streets, but returned to her omega housing hours later. Unscathed. I've asked my police contacts to tell me more, but the omega didn't give them more.

I've been pacing around the house looking for god only knows. I played piano until I annoyed myself. I ignored my emails. I didn't show up to my meetings. I tried to rub one out but couldn't finish (which is making me wonder if I need to be admitted to the hospital). Shadow is hiding from me. That asshole. If Shadow's temperament continues to plague this bond, I will absolutely lose it.

He needs to just fuck her.

That's what I am doing, and look how happy I am!

I grip the hair at the back of my neck and tear it so I can feel something other than this torment.

Where the fuck are they?

I have checked the app we have that shows my pack's location, but I don't have a sensor on Ondine.

I hear Sabbies's truck tires on the gravel, and I shoot out like a bullet on the porch. It's already parked, and Boone is helping my omega out of the truck cab, holding her hand.

"Where the fuck have you been?" My anger is unapologetic.

Boone looks startled, and Sabbies comes around the truck looking like I struck him.

"It's 6 o'clock, Jake. Isn't that when dinner is? You wanted us home for dinner. What's going on?"

He's looking at me like there's some other reason that I'd be upset right now.

I ignore him. I ignore both of them and I rush to my omega. Her skirt sits low on her hips, so I take a second to pull it back up on her waist, adjusting her shirt too, and then check her hair to make sure they didn't fuck it up. It looks fine. I pull her into me and kiss the top of her head. My shoulders relax and my jaw loosens. Thank fuck.

Her arms finally go around me for a small hug. Good god, she was gone too long.

"Is everything ok? Jake, your agitation is so strong."

I tip my head to Sabbies, and a growl comes out. He takes a step back. I've got this little sprite back in my arms. I'm already feeling better. But it's not enough.

"Let's go." I take her hand and pull her into the house.

Sabbies is at my heel. "Wait! Jake, stop and explain yourself!"

I pull her to a stop and turn to him, teeth bared. "You were gone too long!"

"We hit the commuter traffic on the bridge coming back, but we aren't even late!" Sabbies is anxious that I'm mad at him. His anxiety is noted. But he had my omega for hours! Hours! He took her from me, and she's been gone too long!

I turn to Ondine, and without thinking, I use my alpha voice—"*Get upstairs to my room and wait for me. Now!*"

Boone, who I forgot was even there, says, "Wow! Jake! What the fuck? That was unnecessary."

Ondine leaves us to go do as she's told. Because she always does as she's told. I don't even think I needed the alpha voice.

I look at Boone and Sabbies, who have a mix of shock and fear between them.

"I didn't like that one bit. You take my omega from me all day! All day! I had no eyes on her." And then I add, as quickly as possible, "All those missing omegas were taken in the city."

Sabbies garners a quiet voice, like he doesn't want to spook me. "I had eyes on her the whole time. She's ok. Nothing happened."

My attention is split between his wide, earnest eyes and where my omega is waiting for me. Sabbies is my bonded alpha. I can't hurt him any more than I can hurt myself. I take a deep, calming breath. "Wait for us. We will still eat together."

And I practically run into the house after that vanilla cream smell that leads me up to my room at the end of the house. I shed my shirt into the hall and my shoes, and I kick off just as I'm shutting the door. I wrap my arms around her middle and crash us into my bed.

I bury my face in her neck and hair and breathe her in. She smells like a salon. She smells like Boone. I don't like it. I rub my face on her, spreading my scent as much as I can. She parts her legs, so I lie more comfortably between them as I'm crushing her.

"I need you," I growl at her. Her hands stroke my shoulders in a calming manner. "Now."

I pull her skirt up to her waist, crawling down her body until I can put my mouth on her over her pink panties. God, she smells incredible. I move my jaw and work her pussy until she puts her hands in my hair and moans. Her legs squirm, and it makes me just work her harder.

My dick gets so hard.

She's saying something, but I can barely hear it with her thighs pressed into either side of my head. I debate whether to ignore her and keep my ministrations, but my curiosity outweighs it.

I pop my head up. "What're you saying, Omega?"

She looks a bit unglued. So pretty like this. I want to mess her up more. I want her to go to dinner looking disheveled and smelling like me.

"Jake," she says my name on her whispered breath, and my whole body quakes.

"Yes, baby, what do you need?" My hands are roaming under her skirt. Under her shirt. She's not wearing a bra. I need to feel everything.

"Did I do something wrong?"

I stop.

"No, baby. Not at all."

"You were angry."

I climb up her body until I'm hovering over her face. "I'm not angry anymore. Now that I have you. Can I fuck you?"

I pump my hips into hers so she gets the message. So she can feel how hard she's made me. She's all pink and flushed and messy. I reach down and try to take off my pants, and while it's difficult—I don't want to move away from her. I need to be closer to her. I need to crawl into her skin. I want to crack open her chest and wrap myself around her heart.

My pants are off, and I move her panties to the side and push the head of my cock into her. It's sudden, and she screams. I eat up her scream. My mouth over hers. I want all her sounds. They are mine now. I push inside her again in several big thrusts. She's wet and warm and perfect. And mine.

Once I'm fully inside her, I can finally breathe. Calm. A heavenly calm cascades over us. Finally. My mind gives up everything it had been racing through. I can see for the first time in hours. I feel normal again.

"Oh, baby, were you empty without me?" I ask her, knowing the answer. Of course she was. She was probably just as distraught as I was all day. But now she's where she should be, underneath me.

I slowly give her what she needs, causing me to start shaking. She strokes my cheeks with her hands, and I look her in the eyes as I rock in and out of her.

"Baby," I moan. She sighs.

I wrap my arms underneath her and then spin us so I'm on bottom and she's on top. She moves to sit up, but I can't have that. No, I can't have her any further away.

"No," I growl and pull her down so her chest is on my chest.

Then I fuck her. I fuck her like I've never fucked anyone before. I hold her tight and fuck her perfect pussy. She screams her pleasure in my ears, and I'm in heaven. I grip her whole body and rock her in that way that speeds her breathing, makes her start muttering, and eventually she takes over and fucks herself to orgasm. It's gorgeous to see. I want to knot her. But we have to go to dinner.

Boo.

I finish inside her, careful not to disturb her peace she's achieved. I join her in the euphoria soon enough.

I feel good. Oh fuck I feel good.

She feels like the most tender warmth. I can't imagine a more perfect place.

I can feel the tiresome feeling from the bond from Shadow and Sabbies. We've been gone long enough. I kiss this woman's cheek and neck, and then pull out of her.

I'm counting the minutes until I get to fuck her again.

***

Ondine

I tell Jake I need to change, and the bastard makes me promise not to clean myself. He wants them to smell him on me. He's such a scab. But for some reason, the omega in me loves it.

I go to my room and unpack my bag from my apartment. I didn't know I wanted to go home until I was there. All my things are there. My favorite coffee (not coffee because omegas can't have coffee but a similar brew made from cocoa beans), my tweezers, my chair I found at a thrift store, my curtains my parents bought me when I first moved in, my magazines, my sheet music. Here at the Meier house, it's just a room. I slip off the skirt and tank and replace them with my oversized sweats and sweater. Grateful to be back in my clothes.

I sigh and sit on the bed for a minute, gathering my thoughts. I've been worried that my time here will be cut short because Shadow isn't doing anything but asking me about Jake when we are together. But I am enjoying my time more and more with the other alphas. Jake's intense energy is enjoyable to be around. Sebastian and I had a moment earlier that is making me shiver just thinking about.

His hand in my hair. His body pressing me into the door. Fuck me. He's the largest of the three men. His big arms. Orange-y scent. Delicious.

I sigh and play with my hair. I almost, in a fit of pettiness, went shorter. But I actually don't want to upset Jake. I like being the object of his desire right now. It's fun. He's fun. Albeit very self-serving, but that self-serving now includes ensuring I orgasm as much as I have been, then let's go. And I got $500 today. I just can't get too close. I am, after all, only temporary.

I stop on the stairs before I turn into the kitchen, catching them in the middle of a fight. It is obviously about me. Jake is sarcastically saying he's sorry to Shadow. Sebastian is growling. I step down the stairs and stand in the portal, looking into the kitchen.

It smells incredible. Emmerson, the beta, is finishing setting out a lasagna and salad next to plates and cutlery, and a vase of daffodils. He makes eye contact with me, and then suddenly looks at Jake and looks down. Jake doesn't notice, but Emmerson definitely was worried he might be caught giving me attention.

Shadow sees, though. He looks at me and gives me a piercing death glare. I don't look away. I'm too curious. Being in a pack is not as simple as I imagined.

I know it's stupid to have thought it would be simple.

I just thought omegas hung around the house in cute outfits, making bread and gardening or whatever, and then getting railed by several alphas. Maybe I watch too much tv. But no, I've seen omegas before. At the zoo or aquarium. They wear little outfits and are surrounded by smiling alphas. They have flat shoes and no purses. Just vibing. Like well-kept pets.

I assumed they were brainless incubators.

Even thinking this is making me feel like I've got the wrong idea of what I even am.

"I'm going to the gym," Shadow shouts like he'd rather continue fighting, but is too angry. He is still staring at me. And not leaving for the gym. He's dressed for it, though, in black cuffed activewear pants and a green shirt. It makes his amber eyes stand out.

"Shadow, we are eating as a pack, and that's final."

"And who's invited to this pack dinner. Are our betas? Our random alpha *friend*, Boone?" I look around and don't see Boone. I'd thought he left. "Or our time-bomb omega we bought and paid for?"

I frown.

"It'll be the four of us. Emmerson, you can go. And stop looking at my omega." Jake says in a way that makes it obvious why, even though he's the youngest alpha in the room, he's the pack leader.

"She's your omega? Really?" Shadow rolls his eyes. I notice Sebastian in the corner, eyes closed and head hanging down.

"Fuck all the way off," Jake says through gritted teeth.

Emmerson finally darts out the side door. Everyone is at a standstill.

"Everyone, find a seat, now!" Jake says to the room. Sebastian pulls a chair over. Shadow backs up and sits on the counter, and Jake motions for me to sit in the chair nearby. He remains standing.

"What the ever living fuck is going on?"

No one says anything.

"We talked about this months ago. Months. We've been a pack for five years now. And a few months ago, we talked about getting an omega. Shadow was worried he wouldn't like her. Sebastian was worried she wouldn't like us. So we decided to get an Institute placement. A trial." He's talking real slow, like everyone in this room is an idiot. "We drew up our contract, and all of you agreed to the terms." Jake takes a breath. "Shadow, you told me that you were excited. Then

I fucked up, because I couldn't hide my small, not-at-all relevant, personality disorder during the interviews."

What? I just thought he was a bit of a narcissist, but not necessarily in the clinical sense.

He continues, "So, instead of disappointing you, I found us a solution. And here she is. She's young and pretty, and there's seemingly nothing wrong with her"—*gee, thanks, Jake*—"and we all had a lovely time during her heat. What am I missing?"

Shadow and Sebastian are silent.

I resist the urge to ask if we can eat yet.

I'm staring at the giant pan of lasagna on the counter. It looks so bubbly and delicious. How can I make it mine?

Finally, Sebastian says, "I told Shadow that I know he's been depriving the omega of a standard level of care."

Oh.

"I also told him that I have been giving him space to be with Ondine, but since he's not caring for her properly, I would no longer keep my space. I like her," he looks at me, "I like you. I can't be here and see you being deprived." He turns back to Jake. "Shadow is still welcome to do what he wants, but he will now share her among all three of us."

My eyes are so wide, they start to dry out. Sebastian has decided to...care for me? My head is slightly shaking left to right, rejecting this. This isn't happening. He doesn't really mean it.

10

Unguarded

Ondine

J ake's phone rings, and it cuts through the silence like a blade. He looks at who is calling and grits his teeth, points at his pack mates, and says, "We will discuss this more. Give me a minute."

And then he answers his phone and leaves the room.

Sebastian takes the initiative to walk over to the lasagna and cut himself a hearty square. I'm literally salivating. I wipe my mouth as inconspicuously as possible.

Sebastian takes my hands and brings me to the table. He sits me down and puts the lasagna in front of me.

I blink up at him, but he's already gone.

It is such a simple act, but it means so much.

To the uninformed, or someone in this community who's been living under a rock, this may seem harmless, but it's far from it. Alphas have rituals of keeping, caring, and feeding their omegas. These rituals are closely tied to their base selves. It's primal and dead fucking serious.

Jake is their leader, and the message he's been sending when he serves me a plate has been one of acceptance and respect. Now with Sebastian...

It's something you do when courting a mate.

Sebastian ignores the befuddled look from Shadow and fills up a glass of water, then returns to me. He places the glass of water in front of me, pats my arm, and turns back to Shadow.

Sebastian is about to say something, and it's about to be serious, based on the grim look on his face—but Jake returns.

"Pack it up, boys. We just got that call we've been waiting for." Jake makes eye contact with Shadow and Sebastian, and their whole countenance change. They drop all their heat they had for each other and whip into action. They take off to their rooms.

"What's going on?" I say, standing abruptly.

Jake comes up to me, looks me head to toe, then answers, "There's a client with whom we are under contract. We've been waiting for someone to make a move, and he just did. I've got all three of us on private detail. Ten betas. Four fleet vehicles. Our client is due to arrive at the private airport nearby in under an hour."

Sebastian strides into the kitchen wearing a fine black suit, white shirt, and skinny black tie and shoes in hand. Oh, god, he looks fine. Did he look this attractive earlier? He sits on a chair and ties up his shoes, and starts asking questions. "Are we doing my plan? With Shadow and me arriving first? And our secondary team is staying with you and Freddie?"

He stands and hands Jake his tie. Jake pockets his phone and throws the tie over Sebastian's head, then he lifts his collar and ties his tie while answering his question.

"Shadow is staying with me. Because I will be with Alpha Wong. But I like the idea of you being there when we arrive. Let's tech up in the car. We need to get there now. You take the secondary team to the Sky Nest Hotel first, before the restaurant. I've got the tertiary team headed to Crimson Lion now."

Oh my god, I'm such a dimwit. This whole time, I'd been in Jake's office. Listening to all his calls. Hearing him speak about his work. And this is the first time it's dawned on me what they all do. They are private security. This is why they are out on the peninsula. The small airport is out here. They have six black SUVs for chrissake.

There's so much activity around me. Jake finishes Sebastian's tie, patting him on the chest, and they shove some food down quickly, leaving their plates in the sink. Shadow rushes in with his suit and tie already put together. He doesn't bother with dinner and just chugs a protein shake. Jake leaves and returns with bags and hard Pelican cases. Betas on their staff come in and out of the house, asking questions and taking equipment. And before I know it, I'm alone and the house is silent.

I turn in circles, looking around in confusion. From the time of the phone call until now was maybe five minutes. Jake's ominous footfalls make their way through the house to me.

He's typing on his phone before he even says the first word.

"We're going to be gone for two or three days. Maybe longer. We take shifts and will be home at various points. Are you going to be alright here?"

"Um," I don't even know what to say.

"Are you going to be ok?"

"Can I go home?"

"What?" He stops typing.

"You want me to stay here? While you're all gone?"

His mouth hangs open. He looks in two different corners of the room, like answers will be there before facing me again. "Stay here. You're staying here. Don't fucking leave."

I'm not entirely sure what I'm going to do here all alone. I don't do them any good here. And five minutes ago, they were fighting because of my inability to do anything good for Shadow. I am a bad omega.

"I'll call you tonight. Text me. You'll be fine." With that, he grips my arm, but just lets go and leaves out the side door.

As soon as the last car leaves the driveway, my stomach growls. I turn to my food and scream in alarm, "What the hell!" My heart is beating out of my chest, and I think I jumped a whole three feet vertically in the air. "Boone! I didn't realize you were still here!"

Boone is standing by the big picture window in the kitchen, holding the back of my chair. He gives me a sly smirk and gestures for me to sit. I would ignore him or stay clear of him, but I'm so godawfully hungry. Ok, not true, I'd sit just to see where this is going.

I sit down, and he pushes in my chair and then takes the seat to my left.

"You know this exact situation was referenced in your contract," he says with a grin. He's got a great mustache. Just so full and perfect. A mustache that probably makes a lot of men jealous.

"Really?"

"I don't know, Ondine. Did you really not have your lawyer read it before you signed?"

"Why?" I watch as he raises his eyebrows but doesn't answer. "There's nothing in there I should be worried about, right?"

"I guess you'll never know." He winks. I roll my eyes.

I'm so worried I won't get another chance, I dive right into my dinner. And ignore Boone. He makes me feel strange. It's probably just our designations. I feel all tingly, like I've just been electrocuted, but I cannot tell if it's good or bad? Who knows. I don't. All I know is this food is out of control good.

"You like the lasagna?" He asks, like he's teasing me.

"Yes," I answer between bites.

"It's my specialty."

I drop my fork. "You didn't make this. I saw Emmerson setting it out."

He looks a little wounded. "There are two more in the freezer. All mine. I brought them over. Emmerson put it in the oven."

What strange behavior from an alpha. It almost seems like courting behavior. "You feed the Meier Pack?"

He shrugs his shoulders. "On occasion."

I pick my fork back up and finish my food. Boone makes pans of lasagna and puts them in the Meier Pack's freezer. He's so comfortable with them he can be in their house when they aren't home. What is his deal?

"So you're not part of their security business?" I ask, trying to suss him out.

"I help them out here and there."

"With attorney stuff?"

"That. And other things."

I'm too tired for evasive answers. I finish my plate and take it to the sink. He stays at the table while I put everything away. Wipe the counters. Arrange the chairs nicely. And then leave.

I don't want to go to my room, so I play the piano until my fingers ache. Hopefully, the unbonded alpha got lost.

Jake texts me later that night.

> You haven't texted me.

> Was I supposed to?

Yes.

What was I supposed to say?

That you miss me. That you want me home.

It's been two hours.

We are stuck in the city for a few days. The job is not going to be completed quickly.

What's the job exactly?

I'm glad you asked. You never ask about work. Freddie Wong hired our firm to be his personal security while he's in Cash City. His father is Senator Robert Wong. There's been a threat on his life, and Freddie thinks it's Alpha Lee Man-ho that brokered the contract for the threat. Last night, we met Freddie at the airport and escorted him to the meeting with Lee at the Crimson Lion. It got heated, but not violent. Threats were exchanged.

That all sounds very serious. Are you ok?

Yes, and it is serious. We are glued to Freddie while he's here. He's got a reputation for being reckless and operating outside the law. It's my job to just make sure he doesn't get himself killed.

When are you going to bed?

Now.

Send me a picture.

11

Sky Nest

Ondine

I don't know if Boone has left. I can't see the driveway from my window. It overlooks the river. And I haven't ventured too far from my room since last night. Mostly because there's a slight zapping feeling under my skin that I can't help but associate with his presence.

Maybe Jake asked him to stick around and watch me.

I sent Jake a picture last night, and he asked for several more, which I obliged. I was just lying in bed reading through my contract with the Meier Pack. There are expectations, but nothing too alarming. I can't sleep with anyone else but the three pack members. Or do anything they might imagine is cheating. It's vague enough to make me want to be wary. Is that what Boone meant last night?

There are pages in the back for situations that I don't understand. They cross-reference with one another so much it just appears to be legal nonsense. Boone wrote this for them, so I wonder if he wanted to show off all the Latin he learned in law school or something.

This morning, Jake texted again. Saying good morning and asking what I'm doing.

I told him I was doing nothing.

Sebastian also texted. But he asked how I'm doing. I said fine and asked him the same thing. He replied that he was really busy, but if I need anything to call him.

After I brush my teeth and change my clothes, I check my email and my calendar. I canceled all my lessons since before my heat. My backup for the ballet company is fine, continuing on. The recording studio asked me to come in, but I declined. They all know I'm an omega, and this shit just happens.

There's an email from the Cash City Symphony Orchestra. It's a little vague, so I call the number on it.

"Yes, hello, this is Ondine. I received an email about the interim position for a pianist. I am not sure what it is telling me—can you explain?"

A sweet female voice that was previously professional suddenly turns excited. "Oh, Ondine! The omega. Oh my gosh. Yes. So, we have accepted your application and are just trying to schedule an audition time with you. I didn't quite know how to word it. We've never worked with an omega before. I didn't want to type out 'can you tell me when your next heat is' on an email, you know!"

It's a little cringy, for sure. I am trying not to be offended. She's honestly just trying to be accommodating. And this is the opportunity of a lifetime.

"Yeah, no worries. What are the audition dates?"

"Oh! Let me look," she says, and I hear lots of typing and paper shuffling. "We are auditioning the other pianists at the end of next month."

"Oh, that's perfect! That works for my schedule."

Her voice goes even higher, and she tells me that it is so great to hear. She gives me my time and date, and information on dress code and expectations.

It will all come to me in an email later, so I don't take notes.

We end the call.

I would fucking take military grade heat suppressants to make sure I was there, even if it was during my heat. When I applied for the position, I nearly threw up, I was so excited. I cannot believe I got a call back.

They can't discriminate because of my designation, but I can't, as an omega, be fully relied on either. So if I got on with the company, it would be a tandem position with someone else (their current pianist who is pregnant and about to go on leave). It's the perfect opportunity for me. Additionally, not all their performances even have an organ or piano, so it's such a minor role. But it would be incredible. Everyone would know how talented I truly was. I'd forever get to claim the position. And I got an audition.

I feel so prepared, it's stupid. But it helps that Jake's house has a piano.

My fingers twitch on my knees. I walk in circles around my room.

I text Jake back and tell him I'm going to play piano. He asks for a video.

He's so funny. I wonder if the other alphas are wondering why he's been on his phone all morning.

Finally, I leave my room and make my way to the piano room. The sunlight filters in beautifully in this north-facing room. Ever since blooming as an omega, I've become so sensitive to my surroundings. Whoever designed this room deserves a fat kiss. It's not too hot or cold. The light is steady all day. The river flows past, and you can see it from the giant windows. There are like seven different seating choices.

I sit down in front of the piano and get warmed up. Then I prop my phone up and play for a minute or so for Jake.

> That was so beautiful. You are exceptionally talented.

> Now do one with your top off.

I roll my eyes. He's such a perv.

I get lost in my warm-up, playing scales and my favorite bits of music. I don't even move on to my music or any of the things I need to work on. I just repeat over and over again the bridges from my favorite songs, the intros of songs my teacher used to make me play, and then some of my college friends' favorites they'd make me play for them. Each part makes me dip into my memory of all those I've cared about.

After who knows how long, I come back to myself. My back aches, and my fingers just can't play another note.

I'm breathing heavily. My chest expands, taking in long inhales. As I remove my fingers from the keys, my hands shake.

I open my eyes slowly and slump down, turning away from the piano.

"Wow," a deep male voice says from the window seat. I turn around and face the intruder. Boone. He stands and claps for me, slow and loud.

"Boone," I sigh and shake my head, still trying to come back to myself, "What are you doing here?"

He takes a few steps closer to me. "Listening. You play...well."

I turn so he doesn't see me roll my eyes. "Thanks."

"Are you hungry? I can make coffee. Also, scones."

My hands are still shaking. I probably should eat, but the vague lines in the contract about being intimate with other people remind me how dangerous this situation is. I'm alone. And Boone is their friend.

If he wanted to, he could take what he wanted from me, and I would have very little power to reject him.

Despite probably already failing at this placement, I want to succeed. I want the rest of the money. I want to buy a real piano. I want the independence that money can give me. I would be able to be on the Cash City Symphony Orchestra if I could afford to take care of myself entirely.

Additionally, I kind of want to just be part of a pack for these few weeks. Even one like this.

Lastly, I don't want to upset Jake or Sebastian.

I swallow any fears I may have—"No, thank you, Mr. Anderson." (His full government name was on the door to his office, and I noted it when we picked him up yesterday.)

He levels a look at me, a "what the fuck are you on about" look. I don't give him anything back.

"You were friendly to me yesterday. What's changed?"

Now it's my turn to give him an incredulous look. He's not stupid, and neither am I. The silence of this empty house fills the space between us, loud and obvious.

"Ah," he elongates the sound of him figuring it out. Just then, dark clouds edge between the sun and the earth, sending the previously bright room into shade. "You don't trust me. Is that right?"

"I don't know you," I reply too quickly.

"Come have breakfast with me. Get to know me."

"If I told Jake that you and I were here, alone, having breakfast, what might he say?"

Boone's eyes darken, meaning he's tipped his chin down and lost his smile. His jaw is tight. I was right. Boone is up to something.

I cannot have this renegade alpha ruining my time here. I want the money. I want this to go well. What if I want another placement?

I'd need their recommendation. I won't let some cowboy lawyer ruin anything for me.

I grab my phone from atop the piano, but before I can call anyone, Sebastian comes into the front door and sees Boone and I in the piano room.

"Fuck," Boone swears both loud and clear.

***

Shadow

I awake to the crushing weight of four tiny paws upon my chest. My eyes peel open to be greeted by the emerald green eyes of a black and brown striped kitten.

"Princess, get off of him," Freddie Wong, our client and my half-brother, calls to his cat. I pick up the critter by the scruff and stand. Then I hold her in my arms like a baby. She immediately begins to purr louder than anyone might imagine a kitten weighing one pound, soaking wet, would purr.

"Why the fuck did you bring your cat with you?" I mutter as I make my way to the coffeepot. I discard the cat on the edge of the couch. We are staying at the Presidential suite at the Sky Nest Hotel downtown, Cash City. Freddie got the king-sized bed in his own room, and Jake took the other room. I slept on the couch. Sabbies stayed with the beta team down in some rooms we have blocked out. The sun has just started to rise, filling the high-rise hotel room with its obnoxious light.

Freddie pours the last of the coffee into a mug for me and gets to making another pot. He's got a cigarette hanging from his mouth and is shirtless. "I just got her. I couldn't leave her behind. She's mine."

I can't help but think about Ondine back at home. It makes my chest ache.

"Any word from Man-ho?" he asks me. We had him followed last night after the meeting, but we didn't find any unusual behavior.

"Last I heard, he'd gone home. No one left and no one arrived. Doesn't mean anything, though."

Freddie's dad (not my dad) is Senator Wong, and Senator Wong has his fair share of enemies. Man-ho is among the most dangerous. When we first heard of a hired gun attempting to take him out, rifle on a roof and everything, my mother went crazy. She called Freddie absolutely frantic.

Freddie couldn't deny her pleas to come to the city and take care of things. He kind of owes her for making her deal with a lot when he was younger. Our mother had to send him away when he was only 13. He was always picking fights, stealing shit, using his alpha voice on people, and getting into trouble. She sent him off to the Man-ho Alpha School for Boys. But he ran away. He never made it. He was missing for years.

Freddie popped up just a few years ago as this—a less-unhinged, self-possessed man. Still an asshole, though. He found himself at a different sort of school, and they taught him how to focus his feral behavior into something workable.

"I want that fucker flayed and burned." Freddie has his own personal vendetta against Lee Man-ho. Not just this last incident.

"Well, he's got us backed into a corner," I respond. Man-ho kept his hands clean, so there's nothing within the law we can do. But that won't stop Freddie, I'm sure. "What're you going to do?"

"I'm going to beat the shit out of him. What do you think? I was going to organize his workers' rebellion? Come on, little Shadow. We're alphas."

I roll my eyes, but don't let him see. No one can beat Lee Man-ho. He has more alphas surrounding him, loyal to him, than any man in the city.

Jake comes strolling into the main room, eyes glued to his phone screen. "Morning."

He looks unkempt. For Jake. Maybe no one else would notice, but I do. His tie is in his hand and not on his neck. His belt is loose. His shoes look scuffed. Honestly, he's a wreck for Jake.

"Morning, Jake. Any word? I need his location. As soon as he leaves his house, I need to know." Freddie flexes and then shadow-boxes an invisible opponent.

Jake pops his head up, confused for only a moment. He was clearly not doing work on his phone. Was he texting Ondine? I wonder if she's awake.

If I were home, I would know if she was awake. If she's eaten. What she's wearing. How she has her hair done.

"Is Ondine awake?" I ask over my cup of coffee.

Jake pours himself some coffee and looks over at me. "Yeah, she's awake. She sent me some photos last night. I put them in the group chat, didn't you see?" My face flushes hot. Yes, I did see. And yes, I did fucking yank my dick to them.

It's unnerving to feel this attracted to a woman. She'd sent those photos to Jake (and he sent a screenshot of her permission to share them with us), but if I'd asked her, would she have sent different pictures? Ones posed just for me?

"I saw them, but that was last night."

We didn't talk after our blowup last night in our kitchen. Sebastian had come at me in a way I had never seen from him before. He asked me what Ondine and I had been doing during our time together, but he was openly criticizing. He said she was there to help me. I know that's why she is here. I know. But instead of telling him that, or explaining myself, I accused him of being just like Jake, already half-crazed. He didn't deny it.

She's gotten to him, too.

"Well, I'll have her send more this morning if it's so important to you."

Freddie falls down and starts doing push-ups. "Who's Ondine?" His stripey kitten leaps up on his back and holds on as he continues his push-ups.

"Our omega," Jake answers, and I hold still. Watching Freddie for his reaction. He stops midair.

Jake, you fucker.

"Shadow, you have an omega?"

Oh crap. Freddie still lives at the place he wound up 20 years ago. It's a monastery for alphas. He meditates for ten hours a day. Studies martial arts for all the other hours of the day. As far as I know, he's never even spent time with an omega.

He's also six years older than me.

"Freddie, don't make it weird."

"I'm not making it weird." He starts his push-ups again. "When did you bond with an omega?"

I clear my throat. "It's a temporary placement. Two heats."

"Through the Institute?"

Freddie wants to know if us psychopaths qualified for Institute placement. He wants to know for his own sake. If our group of misfortunate renegades got approved for Institute placement, maybe he could do it too.

"We did it privately."

Jake butts in, "Shadow, don't tell your brother our business."

I snap my mouth shut. It wasn't me talking about Ondine's dirty pictures in front of him only moments ago, but whatever.

Jake's phone pings. I can't help but move over to him by the table and look over his shoulder. Ondine is at the piano. Her head resting on the keys. The morning light haloed around her ashy blonde hair. I like her haircut. Her short hair suits her.

I make an accidentally pleasant noise, and Jake responds with his own.

"What?" Freddie asks, coming over to see.

"Freddie, you're paying for our services, not for access to photos of our omega."

Freddie scoffs. "Your omega? Sounds like she'll be a free agent soon enough. Have you thought about what will happen to her then? If she can handle your pack of disturbed, aggressive alphas, that opens up her options. She'll be highly sought after."

My heart sinks. We're running out of time. That's all I can think of suddenly. We don't have any time at all. But I can't let myself be open to her. She'll tear me apart, and it'll be worse than it was with Jake.

Jake waves my half-brother away. "Worry about your own life, Alpha Wong. Don't you have a father to avenge?"

"That and more—" Freddie mutters.

I don't get the chance to ask what he means by that. Sabbies calls in. Man-ho is on the move. Sabbies is handling the team, keeping Man-ho watched. Jake and I are on Freddie duty.

Princess the cat darts up my leg and gets all the way into my hair. She's too cute to be mad about it. And she also starts to purr as soon as she's tangled in my hair.

I grab the back of the chair Jake is sitting in and lean down to his ear. "Did Sabbies like the pictures?" I ask Jake while he's also listening to our pack mate on the other end of the phone. He turns slightly so I can see his smile.

"That's good to hear. Sounds like you got the area covered. What about the photos from last night? Was it enough to keep you warm?"

There's a pause.

"You fucker," I hear from the phone. "Get her to do it again."

"Already on it. Sounds like you got Man-ho all handled for a few hours. Ondine mentioned going back to her apartment instead of staying at our house. If it's not too much trouble, can you burn her apartment to the ground? And then go visit her. Make sure she's well."

Jake asks everything in one deadpan tone. I chuckle and untangle the cat, letting her down to the ground gently.

"On it," Sabbies says.

Jake ends the call.

This is a serious move. Is he planning on trying to keep her?

"You're not serious, are you?"

"As a heart attack, Shadow."

Freddie starts laughing from his place on the floor. A maniacal cackling laugh. "Oh, she's going to fucking suffer for having let you psychos into her life."

I suddenly can't breathe.

12

Arrival

Ondine

I failed to mention earlier how precarious my situation was with Boone. I'm sitting at the piano, and he's towering over me. A hand on the instrument, caging me in slightly as I sit on the bench. His face is close to mine. I can smell the alpha. It is, unfortunately, a nice smell. Like you'd imagine a cowboy might smell, outdoors and wildness.

So when Sebastian came into the house and looked over the entry-way to us, in this position, in the piano room, I panicked. I did not play it cool. I put my hands on Boone's chest and pushed. I pushed with all my strength. It did nothing, and he didn't budge. But now my hands are on him, and we are closer than ever.

And his smile has grown.

Sebastian stomps into the room, and with him comes the distinct smell of campfire.

I drop my hands from Boone's chest and peek around him to see Sebastian. "Why does it smell like fire?" I ask before he can say a word.

He immediately stiffens, and his eyes bug out.

I resume pushing the man away from me. "Boone, get away from me, damnit!"

Boone finally lets up.

"Sebastian," Boone greets, standing next to me. Like it's him and I greeting him.

Sebastian's regular orange smell turns into that whiskey-tinged musk. But he keeps all his emotions off his face. Sebastian normally has a sweet face, but he keeps it neutral as he assesses the room and us in it.

"Boone, I'm going to give you the benefit of the doubt here. Maybe you forgot who we are. Who the Meier pack is. Maybe we've grown complacent in our reminder."

Boone fixes his clothes and puts on an air of cool confidence. "We were just hanging out, Sabbies. You'd left her all alone, and I was doing a service to the Meier pack by keeping the lonely little omega company."

I sigh and look at my exits. There's only one—the French doors that lead out into the hall. Maybe I could sneak out of here. Or throw myself out a window.

Sebastian pretends to think on this. His legs are out wide, hands behind his back, and with him wearing that black suit, he looks so powerful. So sexy. It doesn't hurt anything that Sabbies is so damned attractive. But there's definitely some sort of fire-smoke smell on him. Were they camping?

"Fine, then," he says with some humor. "She's coming back to the Sky Nest. Where she won't be all alone."

My face falls. They were not camping. They've been at Sky Nest. The most expensive and luxurious hotel in Cash City. It's a five-diamond hotel. Only celebrities and the wealthy stay there.

Who are these people?

One hundred thousand dollars for a temporary omega? An entire beta staff. Gorgeous suits. Nice cars. They have a house on the peninsula. Damn, Ondine, you could have done a lot worse.

"You can't bring her onto a job," Boone says, and I can't help but be worried about his statement.

"I can and I will. Boone Anderson, you're being quite duplicitous. Did you think you could form some sort of bond with her while we were away?"

"Don't be silly. I was just messing around."

I gulp as the tension in the air continues to grow.

"Ondine, go pack a bag."

I don't know why I'm resisting, but I sit for longer than he likes, then say, "Jake told me to stay here."

He moves from staring at Boone to looking at me. "Ondine, pack a bag now, or come with me as you are."

He leaves no room for another retort. I stand and go pack. I use the bag I'd just gotten from my place. I throw everything in I can manage. I put on jeans and a bra, tie my shoes, then rush to Sebastian's room where I steal a white button-down shirt hanging in his closet. I put it on, only buttoning some of the higher buttons. I tie off the bottom and roll up the sleeves with the cuffs out. His whiskey orange scent and alpha commands sent my omega side into its primal base self, and unless I'm surrounded by him, I will start panting or moaning in distress.

Being an omega is so weird.

***

The entire drive into the city, Sebastian is twitching. His scent changes again—this time a sweet orange smell. I'm so curious about what's happening to him. But I don't want him to stop. His facial expression is both soft and tight. His hands are moving a lot. He's adjusting his seat and the radio.

Finally, I put my hand on his leg. "Everything ok?"

He changes which hand he has on the steering wheel three times. "You're wearing my shirt."

"Is that ok?"

He licks his lips. "Why mine? Why not Jake's?"

I pull out the bag of peach scones Boone made me take "for the road," and I take one out. I take a bite. I thought they'd be dry, but they are melt-in-your-mouth moist. Good god, these are good.

"I don't know." I finish swallowing my bite. "I let my inner omega just do her thing. I think she likes it when you act possessive around Boone. I think she needed a token of yours after that display."

Sebastian clears his throat, hard. "She is you, right?"

I smile at him. "She is me." But I like to imagine her unexplainable behaviors aren't mine. She's so weird. Sebastian and I sit in comfortable silence the whole drive over the bridge. I watch the high-rise building of Sky Nest come closer and closer. It's one of the tallest buildings in Cash City.

I eat all four peach scones. I didn't even think to offer them to Sebastian. Oh well. His sweet orangey smell fills the car, and I bask in it.

"Those were good," I say to myself.

"There are tons of them in the freezer if you ever want more. Shadow makes them."

My head gives a little shake, out of confusion. I thought Boone made them. He made it seem like he did. I'm about to assume Boone at least took them out for me when Sebastian says, "I did warm them up for my breakfast, but you seem hungry enough."

"Don't lie—you could have stopped me."

He gives me a wry grin.

As we navigate into the city, Sebastian tells me more about the client, Freddie Wong. Shadow's half-brother. He tells me Freddie is from the monastery up the canyon, which I am familiar with. I've never spent time with the monks there, but I've seen them. He tells me he's feral. Something I knew the monastery helps with. He doesn't say it as a warning to me, and I don't take it as one.

We pull into the underground parking and drive to the private car parking for the suites. One of the Meier Protections Group beta agents greets us. He checks our credentials, even though he knows Sebastian. He checks in with the team upstairs, and we are free to go in. We ride the elevator up. And it feels like it goes on forever. I'm not going to lie—I'm a bit excited.

So far, knowing the Meier Pack has brought me nothing but interesting situations. I bump my arm into Sebastian and smile at him. He smiles back, and the elevator fills with sweet orange. He's cute.

The elevator finally arrives at the top floor, revealing a private entrance. The doors open, and I step into the Presidential Suite. It's huge. There's a full-size kitchen. Two living rooms, a full dining table. A baby grand piano, white as snow. And the room is filled with Meier Security Agents. Sebastian takes my bag. There's got to be like twenty people in here.

I'm in a daze as I walk forward. But like I know it before I know it, I snap out of my daze to see Jake pacing by the floor-to-ceiling windows on the phone. There he is. *Mine*, the inner omega says. I rub my chest, urging her to chill out. Jake is in a gray suit, a direct contrast to the sea of black suits in the room. Shadow is on the couch with a laptop on his thighs. He's got an apple in his mouth, taking bites as he types out something. Sebastian puts his hand on my lower back, directing me to the left, but someone catches my eye.

A shirtless man wearing only athletic pants and white socks stares at me from just behind Jake, sitting on the windowsill. He has rogue-ish black hair, half-closed eyes, and he's got a cigarette hanging off his thin, dark lips. He's Chinese. Mixed. Definitely Freddie Wong. Though I pictured he'd be in his hanfu robes and not looking like he stepped out of a 90s street gang film. His gaze is heated and playful. He's got leather cords tied around his wrists and a thick silver chain around his neck. I wonder how he'd like it if I pulled on it tightly.

"Who's that?" I ask, knowing the answer. Sebastian turns to follow my eyes. He pushes harder on my back.

"That's the client. Don't worry about him."

"Sebastian," Freddie calls out in a sing-song voice. The room goes steadily silent. Everyone is looking at Freddie and then at who Freddie is talking to on the other side. Jake turns too, ending his call without a goodbye. Shadow doesn't move, only stops typing and looks at me. "Who do you got there, Alpha Meier?"

I look between Sebastian and Freddie. Fuck, I lean in closer to smell that orangey whiskey scent. It makes my mouth water. Sebastian and his emotions are just irresistible.

He puts his hand around my waist and holds me near him.

Jake doesn't wait. He rushes over to us, dips down, and grabs me by my rib cage, lifting me off my feet and into him. Once I'm up, he wraps his arms securely around me. God, he's strong. For being the shortest and youngest of the Meier pack alphas, he may be the strongest.

"Ondine. Fuck me, I'm so happy you're here." These words are just for me. I know he's got other words for Sebastian. Jake rubs his face and neck on me, scenting me. My hair is being pushed up and down and all over the place as he fawns all over me. He carries me out of the room and to the hallway on the left. We take the first door on the right, and he slams the door shut behind us.

"Fuck you're here. Why are you here?" He's not really asking me. I know this because he's not looking me in the face. Just my body. As he peels the clothes off of me. He takes my shirt off and pushes it into his face, smelling it fully. "Interesting. After I fuck you, you'll wear my shirt"—now he looks at me—"Got it?"

I nod enthusiastically. I hope it makes Sebastian jealous. I want to smell him then. See what that does to him.

I am naked in no time, and Jake throws me onto the bed. I bounce so high, I flail about. He kneels in front of me on the floor, grabs my legs from the back of my knees, and yanks me toward him, pussy right on his mouth. But he just stays there. Murmuring and admiring. I lay back and enjoy this. The room is bright and chilly. Like a hotel room ought to be. Jake's hands cast over my skin softly. I like being worshiped by this man.

He parts my lips and sets his long finger at my entrance. He barely puts any pressure on it, just letting the weight of his finger sink into me, further and further. I can feel myself slicking at his ministrations. His finger is far into me, but he holds it still. With his other hand, he snakes it around my thigh and then presses down above my pussy with his palm. He pushes the hood of my clit up, and when it's prominently on display, he flicks my clit with his tongue. I cry out in pleasure.

Spurred by my outburst, he flicks me over and over again with his tongue. Each time, I get louder and louder. Then he enters a second finger. I'm writhing and moaning at the stretching. Then, when I think I'm at my limit, he fucks me with his fingers and secures my clit with his mouth. "Jake!" I cry out. Either a plea or a curse. He's got my thigh wrapped up, holding my body to his mouth. He's going to make me cum like this. Fuck, it feels so good. Didn't we just fuck yesterday? Why does it feel like we were parted for days, if not weeks? Why does it feel like we have to make up for something?

He's completely attached to me, so when I come, he is right there with me, riding out my pleasure with his mouth and hands.

"Fuck, Jake, that was intense," I pant. He unwinds himself from me and drops his clothes to the ground. He tosses my lithe body around until I'm lying on my stomach, and then he mounts me, my legs between his. I'm so wet back there that it doesn't take him long to be able to push his dick between my closed legs and into my ready pussy. I scream into the mattress. He adjusts himself until he's got a good angle. Every movement sends lust and pleasure to every part of my body. And then he leans down over me, laying his body on my back, and whispers in my ear, "I'll have to kill any man who listens to you cry in pleasure, baby. So be careful of the power of your voice. No man out there will use what he hears to whack off with later. I'd rather see him in the ground."

And before I can react, he ruts into me. I pull down a pillow and bury my face in it. Jake fucks me like a man possessed. He whispers filthy things in my ear until I come undone again underneath him. He's a fucking sex god. When he's had enough playing with me, he comes inside me and lies his tired body over mine.

He wraps the short strands of my hair between his fingers. "You're here. You're mine and you're here."

He massages my body with care and affection. Looking me over for any reason to take care of me. He opens a water bottle and tells me to drink it.

"I have to get back to work, baby. And I have to go yell at Sebastian for bringing you here. Why did he bring you here?"

I finish the bottle and crawl into the cool covers of the king-size bed. "He didn't like seeing me alone with Boone."

Jake stops gathering his clothes. "You were alone with Boone?"

"You left me with him," I remind him.

Under his breath, Jake says, "I suppose I did."

He gets his clothes and dresses himself.

He crawls over top of me, pinning me between the covers and the mattress. He pushes a long kiss to my temple. "Relax, sweet omega. I'll be back later. Is there anything you need?"

"No, just nap time," I say. He kisses me again and lets up.

"Goodbye, my dear."

13

Afternoon Tea

Ondine

I wasn't sure what time it was when I awoke. Or where I was. Or why there were four tiny paws pressing down on my chest, the weight of a two-ton elephant. I had trouble opening my eyes (a sure sign of a long, unplanned midday nap), but when I finally got them open, the room was so bright it hurt.

And there was a black-brown, stripey kitten on me.

"Well, hello, baby," I whisper to the kitty. I don't have any experience with cats, but I've seen others talk to them like this. She likes my voice. I know this because she starts purring as loudly as a school bell. I groan and get myself up. In the chair facing the bed, I find my jeans and one of Jake's button-down shirts laid out for me. I like Jake. He makes me smile. He's so ridiculous.

I put his shirt on, and don't bother with anything else, as it reaches the top of my knees, so it's basically a dress, and walk out into the hall. I don't hear a sound in the suite, so I don't expect to run into anyone.

The little cat weaves through my legs and chases my feet, attacking as she sees fit.

"Can I not walk here?" I admonish the cat. There's a fridge and I open it up, looking for something. I'm feeling depleted. Inside, there are some to-go containers, so I pull them out. There's also an elec-trolyte drink. Score.

The to-go containers have an Indian curry, and it smells pretty spicy, but I'm hungry. I put it on a plate and start the microwave.

Across from the kitchen, down in a sunken room, is the white baby grand piano. It overlooks the city.

My microwave beeps. I take out the hot food and try a few bites. And devour the whole thing. But between that and the drink, I start to feel more awake. And I can't stop staring at the piano.

I didn't bring any of my music. I'm already sitting in front of it, though. I lift the lid and finger the keys. I have some parts of Chopin memorized and itching to come out.

It's midday. No one is around. It shouldn't be a problem.

I don't start out quiet. I start out at concert level. Like I'm racing out of the gate. I'm alone, after all. Full access to this beautiful in-strument that most likely never gets any use. The kitten jumps up and walks up and down the piano's edge. I hit the keys like I'm trying to command them to bend to my will. Chopin's angry and chaotic music floods the suite like a broken dam. I let myself go. God, I love this. This is why I don't fear change. Why I pack my bags at the bend of the course. Why I never resist the call. Because here, I am in the most luxurious hotel in Cash City playing Chopin to the world.

I'm on top of the world.

By the time I'm done, I'm out of breath with a smile wide on my face. My shirt has fallen off my shoulder, exposing my arm.

"God, that was annoying," a female voice says from behind me. I turn to see a couple sitting on the couch. The man's arm around the woman. He's shirtless, with only his underwear on. She's slightly more dressed, wearing a short, loose dress and no shoes. Her hair is mussed, and her legs are tucked underneath her. Her face is giving me disdain and disgust.

I can spot a pick-me from a mile away.

The man's face is emotionless. His eyes are set wide apart, and he has that "crazy eye" look. His lips are thin, and when he opens his mouth, his smile is wide and bright. It's actually too wide and bright, so it borders on insane. He's got roughed up black hair. It's Freddie Wong. Duh.

"Hello," he says to me. Ignoring the woman cuddled up next to him. His voice is deep and sexy. A bedroom voice. She rubs his leg, and he grabs her wrist.

I raise my eyebrows and look around for anyone from Pack Meier. I come up short.

"Hello," I finally reply.

"Who are you?" The girl asks, as obnoxiously rude as you can imagine. I fix my shirt, and the man's eyes track my movements. No one here is particularly dressed.

"She's my half-brother's omega," the man answers for me. Brother? He must mean Shadow. It's easy to see once he says it. Different faces. Same, everything else.

"Ewe," she says, and that's my cue to leave. I cannot stand when people act like immature dicks to people they don't know. She's clearly a beta. Don't ask me how I know. It always feels like I'm being reductive, but it's true. Shadow's brother is an alpha, through and through. His size, his confidence, and his voice all lead to that conclusion.

I close the piano and stand before Freddie tries to stop me. "Don't go. I was enjoying the music."

"Where is Pack Meier? Aren't they supposed to be with you?" I hate having to speak to new people. Especially around this woman who's already champing at the bit to find something to criticize me on. Like she's my mother.

Freddie makes me wait a moment before answering. Making me make eye contact first. "You have a sweet voice, Omega. It's tender."

He says it like I haven't heard it a million times my entire life.

"Ondine. My name is Ondine. And you must be Freddie." I pointedly ignore Miss Loose Dress.

"That I am. Your alphas are close by. After Jake stole you away to fuck you down the hall, we got a tip that the police were releasing the man who tried to kill my father. The man who was hired to kill him. We were able to nab him just as he left the station. Your alphas have the piece of shit now. Getting what information they can out of him."

Aren't the Meier Pack security? Why are they kidnapping people? And then getting information out of them. Perhaps I don't really know what these men do.

I decide just to ask. He seems forthcoming enough. "Is that one of the services you require of them?"

He clicks his tongue and then says, "I would have been there with them, but Cynthia wanted to spend some time with me." He turns to her and smiles, but it's a weird smile. It doesn't look right on his face. "And I can't resist. I haven't seen her in years."

Cynthia preens under his attention. I resist the urge to gag. I have to try really hard because they start making out.

She moans, and he groans.

I try again to make my escape, but Freddie continues to talk to me like he didn't just stop to shove his tongue down this woman's mouth and slide his hand up her dress. "Don't leave. Come join us, Omega."

I shoot him a death glare, but he's not looking at me. He's looking at Cynthia.

"Let's all have some fun together."

"You pig!" She stands up and hits him with a pillow.

Freddie has a shit-eating grin. This is clearly a sore spot for the woman. She hits him again. "I'm leaving, Freddie! You know how much I hate omegas. They are disgusting sex slaves. And she's your brother's!" She hits him a third time and then exits down the hall.

Oh, this is fun.

Love being in the middle of whatever the fuck this is.

I'm staring at him, and he stares back. "I thought you'd been living at a monastery."

He looks surprised. "You don't think monks can fuck?"

I feel like I walked right into that one.

Cynthia comes stomping back from the hallway. She has a blazer on over her dress and is tying on her heels while also trying to walk. She's telling off Freddie for being a pig and a fuck boy, and inconsiderate. And gross. So gross. He's gross for suggesting they have sex with an omega. Apparently, I'm a "sopping wet, brainless half-girl."

I can't even be mad, because there was a time when my friends and I said all those same things about omegas. They don't often talk about it, but they can't always determine if you'll be an omega until you suddenly perfume when you're 21 years old. And then you have to face the fact that you might have been a bitch.

Thankfully, the cat doesn't agree with me, because he uses this time to jump out from behind a chair and scare Cynthia to death. Nearly. I clap my hand over my mouth so I don't burst out laughing.

Freddie doesn't hide his laugh, though.

"Fuck you and fuck your cat!" she shouts on her way out. Thankfully, there's a vestibule by the elevators, so the door closes quickly with her gone.

"God, she's a bitch," Freddie says, but not to me. To himself. He scoops up the cat and praises her for her bravery and prowess. "Come on, Ondine. Let's hang out. I want to talk to you."

God, I don't want to hang out with Freddie Wong. I want to put pants on and maybe go out for a tea. I bet the restaurant here has great tea.

I keep walking away from him.

"Hey, stop," his voice softens, "I'm sorry if I made you uncomfortable."

I tug on the hem of my shirt. He's still making me uncomfortable. "Freddie, I'm not about to get involved in your business."

"I like the way you say my name," his deep and throaty voice is back suddenly.

I roll my eyes and leave the room. I get back to where Jake had me. All three of the Meier alpha's bags are in this room. I put on my pants. Get a proper bra on. Then put Jake's shirt overtop. I brush my hair and put on a touch of makeup. I grab my satchel and head out. Freddie stops me in the hall. He's come from the other way and has clothes on.

"Wait, stop, where are you going?" He nearly grabs my arm.

"To check out the restaurant. I don't know. I'll be back."

"Let me go with you. It'll be my treat."

"I was just going to charge the room anyway, so it will be your treat no matter what."

He widens his grin. His eyes are so wild looking. If you didn't know he was feral, you'd know with that smile.

"I'm definitely coming then."

I shrug. If one more fucking alpha demands my time, I'll...do absolutely nothing about it. Fuck me.

Freddie opens the door for us. Pushes the elevator door button. Leads me in and then leads me out. He nearly takes my hand twice, and I have to jump away. He looks a bit embarrassed but shakes it off.

I've never met a monk. I've heard about the alpha monastery. I know that they brew beer, sell honey, and have a lavender farm. I thought I also heard they vowed against ever being with an omega. Perhaps that's why Freddie's girlfriend is a beta.

I heard about the monastery because it's on the same mountain road as the Liberal Arts college I attended. You can see the signs for the turnoff.

Freddie tells the hostess we'd like a quiet table. I look around the ritzy dining room. It's got lots of alcoves and private rooms. There are mirrors everywhere, making it feel like a maze. The lighting is low, and the noise is muted. The hostess leads us to a couch and chairs in the middle up against the window. It's oddly intimate.

I sit on the couch, and he sits in an armchair, which is slightly above me. The corners of our seats meet.

He orders a coffee. I reach over, without thinking, and pull his watch to me so I can check the time. 4:30 pm. His wrists have stacks of bracelets along with the watch. I wonder if he made them. I let go, but his arm stays. He looks a bit discomforted by my sudden touch. I consider apologizing. I just checked the time, though. So I don't. He finally takes his arm back.

"I'll have a tea. Do you have a list?" I ask the server. She nods and leaves. Returning shortly with the list.

I lean back and look over the list. They have a great selection, including teas with dandelion, which are my favorite. I end up ordering two different teas. A dandelion tea and a raspberry leaf tea. Excited to try them both.

Freddie leans over the armrest. "You're Shadow's omega. I got to admit, I thought he preferred men. Big, self-centered, alpha men."

Freddie is going to be just a joy to spend the late afternoon with, isn't he? He's trying to snuff out my character. And if he gets to talk shit on his brother along the way, then he seems pretty good about that, too.

I cross my legs and get comfortable. The couch is marvelous for that. Jake's button-down shirt falls again off my shoulder. I should maybe button it up a few more buttons. But I don't.

Freddie notices.

"He seemed to enjoy himself during my heat. So maybe he's got lots of preferences you don't know about. How close are you two?"

His eyes leave my shoulder and meet my eyes. "Not that close. Actually. I've been away."

"At the monastery?"

He nods. "It's been twenty years now."

"Wow, that's a long time. What do you do there?"

"I'm learning. In training."

"To brew beer?"

He barks out a laugh. The server returns with our drinks. Freddie dumps a pail of sugar into his coffee. He drinks nearly half the mug in one go. "Have you had their beer?"

"I went to Fair Castle. Of course, I've had your beer."

His smile grows. "A Fair Castle girl," he muses to himself. Of course, he'd know about my college. "A princess."

Fair Castle Liberal Arts College has an unfortunate mascot—a princess. Personally, I think the men love it more than the women who attend. During football games, more men are dressed as yellow-haired maidens than you can imagine.

"So, how does a monk afford all of this?" I refer to the hotel and the splendor of it.

"Monks can be rich," he says, but it's not a great joke. So he offers the truth. "It's not that kind of monastery. It's more of a school." He pauses, and I think he may not continue, but then he adds, "We're training to deal with our feral tendencies." He looks nervous. "That got a reaction out of you. Does that bother you?"

"My parents were both alphas. My mother and my dad. I've heard about alphas who are feral."

"Two alphas? I thought female alphas couldn't have children?"

"It's rare. Very rare. The doctors told her I'd most likely not survive. And they assumed I'd be an alpha. But to their surprise, a very beta baby girl was born." I laugh, but it's not funny.

"Beta?"

Freddie notices my tea has steeped long enough, and since I'm deep in my thoughts, still trying to locate the memory of my parents, he pours my first cup. He drops in a lump of sugar and a spot of cream, then hands me the cup.

"Until a year ago, I'd been registered as a beta. Besides my small size and this voice of mine, I'd been a through-and-through beta. I don't even know where my omega mark is."

Lie. I know *now* where it is. But I was unaware until I perfumed and it became sensitive.

"But the blood tests and scans..." He is leaning over his legs, his body tipped toward me. I take a sip. Damn, this is good tea.

"All beta then I perfumed on the night of my graduation."

"What did your parents think?"

"I don't know. They weren't there. We haven't been close for many years. They have a lot of things going on, and so do I. I wrote them an email. Didn't get a reply for a few weeks. The reply was mostly about how they changed the terms of my trust fund so I'd have access to it now. Which is generous. I use it to pay for rent at my place downtown. If I'm careful, it'll last my whole life."

He smiles. God, that smile. It looks like he's got an agenda. "That's what I'm living off of, too. My trust fund. And investments. But I think mine might be a bit more than yours."

I look around at the chandeliers and marble statues. "Yeah."

"What did you study at Fair Castle?"

"Piano." I smile and he returns it.

"You play beautifully," he tells me, and I wince.

"Do I?"

He cocks his head to the side. "No, I guess not. You play monstrously. Like there's a creature inside you trying to rip its way out."

I beam at him. "Now that, I like to hear."

We both take a beat to drink our drinks. The server brings us a tray of assorted treats and sandwiches. I try a pink cookie with some sort of jelly center. It's too sweet, but I eat it anyway.

"So tell me, Freddie, why does this Man-ho want your father dead?"

Freddie's eyes darken. He swallows hard. "I don't know. But I know I want Man-ho dead."

"You have history?"

"Yes, we do. But it doesn't involve my father. It doesn't involve the Senator or these large schemes."

"What do a monk and a local businessman have in common?" I'm trying to be charming, but he is getting more and more serious.

"What do you know about Lee Man-ho?"

"I see his name on businesses. I've heard he owns restaurants and bars. And I think there's a martial arts school or something."

"Or something."

That's it then. The school.

"I passed by it once on my way to the gardens. It has a beautiful archway. Tall stone walls. I don't know what's behind it." I don't even remember the sign on the gate. It's near the central gardens of Cash City. Acreages of reserved land for parks and pathways. There are giant ancient trees, little streams, and bridges.

"The Man-ho School for Adolescent Alpha Boys."

"What happens there, Freddie?"

"Hm?" He wasn't listening.

"Did you go to that school?"

"No."

"What goes on there?"

Freddie pushes all his air out of his lungs, then fills them again fully. Like he's trying to lower his heart rate. "I was 13 when my parents were done with me. I couldn't help my nature. I was unruly. I didn't listen. I stole. A lot. I was violent. I handled most interactions with my fists or my alpha bark. My mother was sick of it. She called the school and had me escorted there. She was adamant it would fix me. I didn't want to go."

"Why?" I ask, but it feels rude. Like I'm being too nosey.

"I often walked by, like you had, on my way to the gardens. I'd seen the boys coming and going, and do you know what I started to notice?"

"What?" I barely say above a breath.

"Broken. They were broken."

"Their spirits?"

He smiles, showing all his teeth. "Yeah, that too. Their bones. Broken arms. Limping. Black eyes. Tender stomachs. I'd watch these kids coming and going, broken. I knew if my mother sent me there, I'd break too. And I'd seen Man-ho's eyes watching me. Like he was hungry. I'd never been afraid until that day, when one of his goons took me out of my home. Took me to the school."

My stomach sours. I look down at my cold tea. I set it on the table and wipe my palms on my jeans. "Do you want to know more? You seem upset."

I look up at him. I feel this buzzing in the air between us. Like I've known him for much longer than just today. "I want to know what happened next. But if you don't feel comfortable..."

"I feel very comfortable with you. Is this just how alphas feel around an omega?"

Is it?

"I never asked an alpha how he feels around me."

He smirks at me and then finishes his coffee, setting his mug down next to my cup. He pours me hot tea from the pot, then hands me the cup so I don't have to reach for it myself.

"So what happened?"

"I fought my way out. I beat the shit out of their handler. But Man-ho himself found me. It was raining that day. He offered me a dry place. A hot drink. An ear to listen to. He wasn't the monster I imagined, so I went with him. He sat me down in his office. In *his* chair. He told me things that would make any young boy excited. He told me what they were doing at that school. He offered me everything. He offered me magic."

A steady stream of adrenaline pumps into me at this story. What did Man-ho tell him? Why does Freddie look so afraid?

"But you rejected him?"

"Yes."

"Why?"

"He looked too excited. I realized he needed me. He needed all these boys. He wasn't telling the whole story. No one, not even my parents, offered me what I wanted. I wasn't dumb enough to believe in his good nature. There's no such thing as fairy godparents. I didn't believe him. Even with his kind, grandfather eyes and his perfectly made hot cocoa. He was warm and welcoming and told me everything I wanted to hear. I called bullshit."

"What did he offer you?" I drink all my tea, so Freddie takes my cup from me. Our hands brushing. "He told me about *primeval lusus naturae*. It's a fancy way to say that he wanted me to accept my feral nature. Give it to him."

I want to know more. I want to know everything. His dark oil slick eyes lock with mine. It feels like magic between us.

But I don't get a chance to ask him more. Jake, Shadow, and Sebastian come into the dining room. Freddie looks over my head, and I turn to see them at the host stand. They spot us and come over. Jake kisses my cheek and then sits across from me. Sebastian sits next to me. Shadow on a chair across from Freddie. Then I notice Jake's bloody knuckles.

14

Treats

Sebastian

She's wearing Jake's shirt. What happened to mine? This is fucking stupid. I tug on it. She looks over at me, first confused, and then she gets my silent question. She leans over and whispers in my ear, "Jake took yours away and left his." And she says, because she's trying to kill me, "What're you going to do about it?"

I quickly show her the white rose I bought from the stand outside the hotel on our way in. She's very confused and quite shocked. I wink as I set it on the coffee table in front of her. It has a little ribbon tied around it, so hopefully it looks like a gift and not like I swiped it from somewhere.

Freddie shoots me a look. Wait, what're we all talking about?

Jake is saying something, "He was told to kill him. By any means necessary. It wasn't a scare or a smoke alarm. He said the man who paid him wanted Senator Wong dead."

Oh yeah, the guy. The assassin. Fuck, that took all afternoon. Jake beat the guy to a pulp. Shadow watched from the...shadows. And I had to keep everyone fucking focused. Jake was screaming at him about god knows what.

But we found out some things. Like, how Freddie's dad was worth only $50,000 for the hit. Kind of low if you ask me. Also, this guy seemed a bit new. He had the artillery, sure, but he had no military background. Maybe not a great candidate for a hit.

We also learned that this guy fucking hates Senator Wong.

"He was no fan of your father, Freddie," Jake was saying. I lean over and smell my omega. Not my omega. And she smells like Jake. He's all over her.

"He had lots to say on the matter. He kept saying that Senator Wong wasn't a real Chinese man. That he didn't take care of his own people. That he's no better than a white man."

Freddie huffs. "That's stupid. My dad has been a leader in helping the Chinese community in this city. For fuck's sake, we've contributed more to the development of Chinatown than any other family."

"Yeah, I wouldn't argue with him. He seemed a few pumpkins short of a patch, if you know what I mean."

I need to rub my smell on her. I don't like that she only smells like Jake.

I look over at Freddie, and he appears like he knows what I'm thinking, with one raised eyebrow. I roll my eyes at him and wave down the server and ask for a water. I'd like a whiskey, but I'm still technically on the job. Jake orders an iced tea. Shadow doesn't say a word. He doesn't look good. His skin is ashy, and his eyes are sunken. I order him a Coke.

We still have to figure out how to help him. But I don't think spending more time with Ondine is going to help at this point.

I reach down and pick up a yellow cookie. Ondine stops me and takes the cookie from my hand. That's my cookie. Why can't I have a cookie? She sets it down and picks up an orange cookie, then puts that in my palm. I lean back with my orange cookie, wholly confused.

"What did you do with him?" Freddie asks.

Jake answers, "Dropped him off at the front door of the hospital. If we need him again, we'll find him."

Jake is watching me and my cookie.

I take a bite. It's nice and orange-y. I look to Ondine for answers, and I just see a self-satisfied look on her face. She picks up the rose and smells it, then sets it back down.

Everyone holds a collective breath.

Oh god, what is this feeling? There's like a balloon inflating in my chest. But it feels really good. Like a good balloon.

Today has been a long ass day. It began with going to Ondine's apartment and starting that fire. I ensured it would only affect her unit. I'm not a monster. I closed all the doors too, so it ultimately was just the kitchen and living room—including that fucking beanbag chair. I also have some boxes of her things in the back of my truck. Including the most random items I thought she may miss, like a comb I found under her pillow.

I "repaired" her thermostat incorrectly, and it started the fire. I wanted to make sure it didn't look like arson. If I weren't worried about arson, I would have doused that beanbag chair with gasoline. But I didn't want anything to connect back to Jake. I also didn't want it to look like her fault. A faulty thermostat is right there in the responsibility of the landlady.

Jake interrupts Freddie, who had been talking about Senator Wong's untarnished reputation with the Chinese community in the city, to address Ondine. "Baby, which cookie can I have?"

"Excuse me?" She asks, and I can't tell if she's making her voice extra sweet or if that's just how she is.

Freddie rolls his eyes and sinks back into his chair. His hand goes to the chain on his neck to play around with. Ondine notices the chain, too. I don't like that look she has on her face as she watches him.

"You gave Sabbies a cookie. Give me one."

Ondine gives Jake her full attention. He's acting jealous. Of a cookie.

"You don't get a cookie."

"Excuse me?" he repeats her question back to her.

The corner of her mouth lifts in humor. She's teasing him. She leans forward and looks over the silver tower of treats. "You're not a cookie guy, don't pretend otherwise."

I'm trying to think if that's true.

Ondine stands up. She leans over, reaching for a small treat. A petit four. It's light pink with some frosting leaves on top next to a frosting pink flower. She picks it up and walks around the low coffee table. What is she up to? I look to Shadow, who hasn't touched his Coke. He's staring at Ondine.

I try to feel what he's feeling, but he has his side of the bond locked down. Shadow knows I'm questioning him, but doesn't want to open up.

She stands between Jake's spread legs. He looks up at her, waiting to see what she's doing. She turns and sits down, right in his lap. She curls up in him, and he puts his arm around the back of her, holding her on him. God. Now I'm jealous.

"You are a cake guy." She holds out the petit four, and Jake leans his head down, taking this little cake into his mouth. He chews and smiles at her. I guess he's a tiny cake guy. I've never seen him smile this big.

"You also need medical attention," she says, and she takes his hand, inspecting his knuckles. He shrugs as he swallows his treat. She looks around for the server, who is quick to come talk to her. "Do you have an ice pack?"

"I will get you something," she says and leaves.

"You're going to take care of me?" he asks, barely above a whisper. That must be the final straw for Shadow because he makes a grisly noise and stands up.

"I'm going for a swim. I'll be done for my next shift."

Jake whips his head to him. "Stop, wait."

Shadow heaves a breath. "What?"

"Take Ondine with you. Freddie and I need to talk about his interrogation from earlier."

Oh yeah, wasn't Freddie supposed to be with that obnoxious woman...what's her name? Sarah? Cecilia? Sophia?

Shadow doesn't respond for several pregnant moments. Finally, he asks, "Wasn't Freddie supposed to still be with her now?"

Jake turns to Freddie, who shrugs. "I got all I needed. Plus, she was rude to your omega. So, I had to send her away earlier."

Jake's eyes pop out of his head. "How on earth did Cynthia meet Ondine? You said you were going to her place. Sabbies, did you know he was here?" And to back Freddie asks, "Were you fucking her in the suite with Ondine there?"

"I had three men with Freddie. I didn't get a debrief from them yet."

They must still be in the hotel. I got distracted by the idea of seeing her again. I didn't even check in. I check my chats and see that yes, the guys I had on Freddie are nearby, and I can see them.

Damn.

Freddie waves his hand like it's no big deal. "The suite is big enough for several activities."

Jake grips onto Ondine tightly. "But you just said she was rude to Ondine."

Shadow takes this distraction to slink away. But Jake catches him. "*Shadow*, I'm not fucking around."

He puts an alpha bark into his voice. Shadow can't not stop and wait. If he resisted him, it would be in direct violation of Jake as our pack lead. He'd be challenging his leadership. It surprises me that I wonder if he'll try. His attitude and behavior lately don't give me much faith in his ability to contest Jake.

But he doesn't. He waits.

Freddie offers an explanation. "Your omega was playing piano like a fiend. She gave Cynthia and I a private concert."

Ondine rolls her eyes. "I thought I was alone."

Freddie offers no more information. Jake puts his hand on Ondine's cheek, moving her face to look at him. "You're ok. Cynthia is a rat. I don't want you near her."

I want to laugh. Jake and his quark, where he doesn't ask someone how they feel, he just assigns a feeling to you, and you have to accept.

"Ondine?" I ask gently, a smile on my lips. "*Are* you alright?"

She matches my smile and nods.

I can feel Jake through the bond, thanking me. It must have been a pretty powerful emotion to get through. Our bond has been stressed because of Shadow.

I haven't felt much beyond anger and frustration in months. The only reprieve was when we first brought Ondine home. Those days when she was in heat.

Jake strokes Ondine's cheek and brings her face back to his. He brings their lips together and kisses her. It's quick. He kisses her cheeks, her eyelids, and forehead.

"Ok, my dear, go swim with Shadow. We will meet up later tonight."

"I don't have a swimsuit."

"There's a shop here in the hotel. Shadow will help you." That last line was meant for Shadow and was said in a lower, serious tone.

She kisses his cheek and stands up. She looks at Freddie, for what I don't know, then offers me a little smile and quick nod, which I return. She then turns to Shadow. He grits his teeth but motions for her to follow him.

Does it make me a bad pack mate that I have this bad feeling?

The three of us seem to share this nonsensical thought because we sit in silence for a while. The server returns with an ice pack and hands it to Jake.

He and I make eye contact.

"I'll go take care of what I need to. And then go check on them." I stand. I'm sure everything will be fine. I need to check in with my people, and then I will check in on Shadow and Ondine. I am sure it will be fine.

15

The Hot Tub

Ondine

S hadow radiates don't-talk-to-me energy. It's a marvel he's able to keep it together.

I don't know how anyone would want to bond with this guy. He's such a fucking mess. His hair looks like he's ripped some of it out. His nails are all broken. The shadows under his eyes are so dark they look purple.

He walks with a noticeable side-to-side motion like a creature might lumber about. It's honestly so sad. No wonder his alphas wanted to do everything they could to make him better. I just want to hug him, but he'd probably growl at me or something. Like a wounded dog.

And that's really what he is, isn't he? Someone who is hurting and clearly in pain.

I follow Shadow to the little shop by the front desk. There's a man in a suit behind the counter in the shop. There are clothes, suitcases, and other items one might have forgotten to purchase on a trip. I go to the rack of swimsuits and look at the price tags, and nearly choke. Good god, this is obscene. I could buy a whole couch or semester tuition for the cost of one of these. I pick out a turquoise one-piece with a really low back.

Shadow purchases it and hands me my shopping bag. He asks how to get to the pool, and I stand at his side. We take the elevator to the private pool meant only for those in high number suites.

There are locker rooms with showers. One for men and one for women. When I enter the Women's Room, I find a very pregnant omega trying to put her panties on, and she's not doing a great job at it.

"Oh, my god, I'm so sorry," she says as she hops around and then gives up before she has a fall. Her hand slams onto a locker nearby to help steady herself. "God, I'm so naked."

I can't help but laugh. She looks very tired and very sweaty. She has long blonde hair. She's petite and has a rack on her that is to die for.

Her big baby blue eyes meet mine, and she gives me the most exhausting sigh I've ever heard.

"Are you ok?" I ask.

She sighs again. "I insisted on coming here for one last fun trip before the babies get here, but I'm getting humbled by the minute."

Her panties hang from her hand as she waves them around.

"Where are you visiting from?" I decide she probably needs to talk more than she needs me to help her get her underwear on. I put my bag down and start undressing.

"Garden Park. One of my alpha's family is from Cash City. But his father is a dick and his mom is a huge bitch, so it's really been just the best time!"

"I don't doubt it. How many alphas are yours?"

She looks at me strangely. "That's widely known as a rude question, you know. But I'm so happy to get to talk about my idiot men, let's just look past it."

"Well, ok." I take the tags off my suit and step into it.

"I have four alphas. And I love them all. We bonded not too long ago. We only got two heats together before I became pregnant. I'm going to have triplets. The guys are so damned excited."

I nod, a little bored. Glad this pretty little omega has four amazing alphas that take her to fancy hotels on vacation and knock her up with a million babies.

I'll most likely never see this person again a day in my life, and I don't often have chances to talk to omegas, so I just ask her what I want to know—"Did you all immediately fall for each other or was it tough in the beginning?"

She looks up at me. Panties still in hand, leaning with all her weight into the locker doors. "No, it was a shit show. Four alphas? Are you kidding me? Listen, have you ever met two men you can rub together who are mentally stable? No. Just don't expect them to be fully formed and perfect. As long as they listen and try, that's enough."

"Yeah, that makes sense."

"I mean, omegas are designed to be with alphas. And we need them. But they need us just as bad. They are just pure chaos without us. We level them. So, of course, it's going to be a wild ride at the beginning. Some of them reject that peace. Some of them are scared. Alphas are emotional teddy bears at the end of the day, truly."

Emotional teddy bears? Is that all Shadow is? Just a scared, apprehensive, chaotic alpha?

"And time helps?"

"Time. Fucking. Scenting. And any primal act, like feeding or caring. One of my alphas got really bad migraines, and I was able to help with them. He follows me around like we are leashed together now. Actually, can you go get him? There's no way I can dress myself. An hour in the pool wiped me out. His name is Buster. He's just out there?"

"Yeah. For sure. Thanks for talking with me."

"Ashlynn," she says.

"Ondine," I tell her.

We smile at each other. She puts her forehead on the locker, and I take that as my cue to leave. The pool area is awe-inspiring. It's all indoors, but the glass walls look out over the city. There is a terrace on the other side, but it's closed off. Probably from the wind. There is a large rectangular pool and two hot tubs surrounded by real palm trees and other tropical spiky shrubbery. There are only two people here. Ashlynn's alpha, I'm guessing, and Shadow, who is swimming laps.

I don't even need to say anything to Buster. As soon as we make eye contact, he's on his feet, running past me into the locker room after his omega.

Just like Jake, I think.

Is that why he jumps at the sight of me? Because I helped him...I don't remember helping him. Maybe he was just lonely. He wants me with him all the time.

And that makes me think perhaps Shadow is lonely. A hurt, lonely dog.

I shake my head. Come on, Ondine. Let's try to take some of Ashlynn's advice. Let's give him some care and attention. He and I just haven't had a chance. The thing is, I am actually starting to like Jake. I wouldn't mind him being my alpha. But Jake already has a pack—Shadow and Sebastian. Sebastian is growing on me. The sweet smell of the rose he brought me comes into my memory. I left the flower downstairs.

I step up to the pool and watch him kick off the wall for another lap.

A good omega is good for her pack (I decide). I want to finish this placement to get my money. And I want to be a good omega.

My time with this pack is finite. And while I got them, I'm going to try all I can to be a good omega. Might as well? I'm being paid very well and not being treated horribly. In no time, I will be back at my apartment. Back to my old life.

Might as well dive in headfirst.

Metaphorically, of course.

I sit on the edge of the pool and watch Shadow with his laps. He does a few more after he notices me. Finally, he stops near me.

"You're just going to watch?" He says as he wipes the water droplets off his face. His cute droopy eyes and gaunt cheeks, now dripping wet.

I decide his question doesn't need an answer. "Do you want to go to the hot tub with me?"

He sighs and rubs his chest. "Sure," he agrees, but then dips back into the water for another lap. Not sure if he wants me to wait, but I don't want to, so I get up and pick the hot tub in the corner.

***

Shadow

It's upsetting how much better the ache in my chest feels with Ondine here and no longer at the house. It's almost as upsetting as seeing her give Sabbies a cookie and sit in Jake's lap.

I hate that she's here, and every day she burrows further and further into my pack. And in my chest.

I pull myself out of the pool and head over to the hot tub. It's surrounded by live trees and plants in some kind of tropical paradise simulation. Ondine sits on the edge with only her feet in the water.

She looks so pretty, leaning over the water, with her back exposed. I never thought I liked women with short hair, but being able to see her long neck and bare back is definitely an advantage.

She turns her face to me as I approach.

"I don't know how to turn the bubbles on."

I look around until I see a large red button on a privacy wall. It's either an emergency button or the button to turn the jets on. I press it without worrying about which one.

The jets turn on, and she makes little "ooo" and "awe" noises.

I hide my smile as I sit down on the edge opposite her. She sinks down into the tub, the water covering her to her collarbone.

We sit in silence for a while. I'm a little impressed by how comfortable it is. I look her over, noticing her orange-tinted lips, half-closed eyes, and pale blonde hair. I notice how her brightly colored suit matches the water and scenery. The chlorine dances in the air when the bubbles pop, irritating my nose. It's warm and quiet in here.

I'm the one to break the silence. "Were you going to give me a cookie? Or a little cake?"

I keep going over the exchange in my mind.

She smiles at me. "Is a Fig Newton a cookie?"

A Fig Newton? "Is that what you would have given me? Why?"

She laughs. It's small and teasing.

"You three are so silly. I'll let you figure it out."

Oh, she thinks it should be obvious. Let's piece it together. She gave Sabbies an orange cookie. Jake a little cake. I would have gotten a Fig Newton. Is there some sort of cookie language I don't know? Like how flowers have meanings.

I always associated Jake with cake, though. That made sense to me. It's probably because he smells like...

"Oh," I say aloud.

"You got it now?"

"Sabbies's scent is orange. Jake is like a birthday cake. And I've been told I smell like a fig." I rub my chest. "I didn't realize you clocked us."

"I'm an omega. I think it's what we do."

There's this little seed inside me that takes root.

Before I can finish thinking through this strange new development, Ondine asks, "Did you want to fool around?"

"Excuse me?"

She shrugs, and her cheeks go pink.

"Aren't I here for that? Jake brought me here for you, but you don't seem interested in letting me take care of you."

I cast my hands over my face, trying to wipe away the water droplets, only to get my face more wet. She's right. She's here to fix my hormones, as Jake ordered.

"What would the harm be in letting me try?"

She takes a gamble and pushes off the edge of the hot tub, swimming up to me. She's in front of my legs, staring up at me.

I'm in danger.

She sets her hands carefully on my knees.

I have to open my mouth to breathe, otherwise, I think I may pass out.

Being with her during her heat was easy, admittedly. I let the alpha in me come out. And she was a stranger, so she could be anything I wanted her to be. And at the time, she was just a gift from my alpha.

This is different. I know things about her now. I know she has a storm behind her eyes. I know she can hold her own against Jake. I know she can see me when I see her. We are on the same playing field, meeting as equals.

I can't let her kiss me. She'll ruin me.

Just like Jake did.

"Shadow?" she asks to get me out of my spiral. "You're spinning out. Take a deep breath."

I suck in a breath and ease it out.

"Do you want to talk about it?"

They are such simple words, but they feel so revolutionary. Do I want to talk about it? My face collapses in anguish. She leans into me, and I bring my forehead close to hers. I can't touch her, though.

"Talk to me. Tell me about it."

"I can't do *temporary*. Not again."

She stays perfectly still.

"Oh."

I nearly laugh. "Your heat...I was just being a good alpha for you. You were completely out of it, and I was helping you. It would be different now. And I don't know if I can make love to you now, and then watch you walk away."

I can say it with my eyes closed, so I hold them shut and say, "It's awful to watch Jake enjoy you so much. Fearlessly. I just keep thinking how bad it's going to be when you walk away from us."

She makes a little "oh" sound this time, the word not quite forming. My entire body is filled with adrenaline from my fear. I cannot believe I'm saying these things out loud. It's this private little space. This white noise from all the jets. It feels otherworldly. It's her body heat between my legs.

I bring our foreheads to touch, then whisper, "I don't think I could do that. Have you and then lose you. I did it with Jake, and I could only pretend for so long it was ok. We are running out of time, and I'm torn between opening myself to you or shutting you out completely, and I don't know which one will hurt more. Which will kill me first."

And because she's listening and absorbing every word I give her—folding it and keeping it safe—I say, "And the more you are around, the more I'd like to keep you."

She leans in a bit more, pressing more of us together. My bones are quaking, but I stay utterly still. I can't even breathe. Her hands ease up my thighs until her hips are in between my legs. I can feel the heat of her. Solid and real. I'm already leaning down to meet her lips as she stands up taller on her tippy toes.

I let the kiss happen, I might say, but that's not true. I push into her lips, wanting it. Wanting it and yet scared out of my mind.

She's too fucking nice. Her lips are nice. Her smell is nice. Her words are a balm.

Our tongues touch at the same time. She pushes up off my thighs and deepens our kiss. I get hard, and I want to feel between her legs, to see if she's turned on too. It's a spectacular nightmare.

So, that's why, when we pull back for a breath, and her hands come up to grab me around the neck, and even though she's giving me "what's the worst that can happen" eyes, I use my alpha voice on her.

"*Ondine,*" I say, and her eyes blow wide with shock. "*Be still.*"

The Wong brothers were both born with a defect in our voices. Both of us have an abnormally powerful alpha bark. It's strong, my brother could command my father when he was only 9 years old. It's why they tried to send him away. Mine has never had a use. I never wanted to control someone. Until I went to the military academy and they found a lot of use for me.

So using it on Ondine is cruel. And I'm a coward. She's completely still. Her chest isn't rising to take a breath. Her eyes are not blinking. But I'm shaking in her arms.

"*Ondine, breathe, my love.*"

She takes in a breath. Tears escape out of the corners of her eyes. I lick them off her face.

"*Blink, please,*" I whisper. Her shoulders relax, and she resumes some normal function. I press our foreheads together and just breathe along with her.

"I want to kiss you. I want to make love. I want to lie with you in my arms all night. Watching you and following you all day like a phantom is not enough. Ondine, I'm a hungry alpha. I want it all. I don't want a temporary placement. I want to consume you entirely."

But I don't take any more from her. I release my hold on her, and then I carefully move up and away from her.

"I'm sorry."

And then I leave her all alone.

16
Mother

Jake

Shadow might be fucking Ondine. His lust and drama are flooding our bond. While his is intense and prominent, Sabbies is full of worry. What the fuck would he be worried about?

Freddie is talking about Cynthia. Anytime he has to see her, he complains about the experience for days and days. Cynthia is a personal administrative assistant for Man-ho. She mainly runs his calendar. Freddie has had a casual thing with her for years. Basically, every time he comes into the city. And she has loose lips, so it works for our benefit.

He hasn't said anything of value, though. He's just detailing all the things he does not like about her: her grating voice, her sticky skin, her snapping jaws. I feel like I'm the one who slept with her by this point.

"And she's so full of shit. We were listening to Ondine play this incredibly erotic and emotional song on the piano, and her reaction was to pretend it was annoying. I've never wanted to punch a girl before that moment, I swear."

I don't like my omega's name on Freddie's lips. I growl at him, and he stops talking. I pull out my phone and text Sabbies.

"Why are you so damned worried? They are together. It's a good thing."

Freddie is thankfully still silent. I huff out an annoyed breath and look over at him, fiddling with the chain around his neck.

Sabbies doesn't text back, but I see he's read my text. Who would have thought being a pack leader to only two alphas would amount to this much drama?

"Freddie, I need your opinion," I say. Freddie has always been a good ally. He makes good decisions. He's strong. He's independent and intelligent. He's also been part of a monastery that swears off omegas or whatever the fuck they do. "Do you think an omega is good for a pack?"

Freddie stops playing with his necklace. He weighs his answer carefully. I appreciate him taking the time to answer. "Good for a pack?" He rolls the question around in his mouth. "Jake, they are the pack. They are like tiny suns begging for us to orbit them."

"This is what they say at the monastery?"

"Yeah, they say that in the beginning, when all we were undefined ancient humans in a hostile world, trying to survive long enough to procreate, we *had* to form packs. We needed alphas to protect, and betas for their wisdom and skills, and we surrounded our most treasured prize—the omega. At the monastery, we learned that an omega is a death to the alpha's feral self. We were never supposed to be without her. We've moved so far away from that."

I've heard it all before. How modernity has made being an alpha very difficult because there is hardly any need for our specialities anymore. And instead of adapting, many alphas just kick a fit at the world for no longer being the place for them.

"So, then you'd say having an omega fixes all of that?"

"It's more than just 'having' her, Jake. Let me tell a story," he says, and I sigh, then wave his story on. "Last year, I was on a hiking trip. Solo. As I've done many times. I was in the river, washing my feet, and drinking what I could before heading off again when I heard a group of college coeds having a bonfire nearby. I hid from them and just watched. Most were wearing their mascot costumes since they'd come from a big game. They drank beer, ironically, from the monastery brewery. They danced and listened to loud music. One woman, an omega, was wearing this insane costume. She had a wig of long yellow yarn. She had a medieval pink princess dress that went past her hands and to the forest floor. She had all this silly makeup on that made her lips look round and her cheeks bright pink."

"Freddie, can you get to the point? You hooked up with the princess, and she rejected you. There I did it for you."

I shake my phone, willing Sabbies to text me back. He doesn't.

I drop my head back and scoot down into my seat. Shadow's lust, that floods the bond, is all scraggly and missing pieces.

"We didn't hook up, Jake. We connected. It was like I'd never seen the stars at night or a fucking flower bloom. Smelling her on the wind sent me into a panic. She was like this missing piece of everything I'd never been. I knew that if I were to just make her laugh or even sigh with contentment that I would finally achieve what the monastery had been trying to teach me."

This makes me put my phone down.

Not because he was telling the story in any way that made me think he'd get to the point, but because he was speaking about something I'd been curious about. The omega-craze. How absolutely mad Ondine was making me. All my thoughts had Ondine at the beginning, middle, and end. It was like she carried a piece of me wherever she went, and I wanted to be united with it anytime we were apart.

"What happened with the girl? Why aren't you with her?"

"I was shocked. And scared. I didn't think I could ever be worthy of an omega. I left her with her friends and returned to the monastery. I had never even imagined being an alpha that has an omega. I needed time. But I had nightmares every night. I regressed all my progress with my studies. They sent me to the hospital, where I was diagnosed with 'bond sickness.' I didn't even hear her speak! It took weeks to recover without her. I had to go through scent therapy. I still take drugs for it today."

I blow out all the breath from my lungs, so I don't have any left to tell Freddie that he's a fool for leaving her behind.

"You don't know who she was?"

"My alpha leader told me something interesting. He told me I may have met my scent match. Have you heard about it, not in tv shows or movies, but in real life? Someone fated to be yours? I figured if that was true, she'd find her way back to me. And..." he stopped his sentence abruptly.

A scent match. How very cool and unique, just like Freddie. I'm not sure if I buy it. He sees a princess in the woods and nearly dies. How dramatic.

I shake my phone again like it's a damned Etch-A-Sketch.

My knee is bouncing, and I need to know what's going on with my pack.

"Freddie. This is all troubling information that I don't know what to do with. I hope you find your princess omega scent mate who will do whatever, whatever, whatever. Or she finds someone else and moves on. I'm going to find the pool now."

I stand up and fix my suit, and then button my suit jacket. I nod to Freddie, who doesn't seem to mind my speech, and turn to leave. But Sabbies is standing right there, and next to him is a small Chinese woman. She looks to be in her fifties, and she's wearing very stylish clothes. Oh my god, it's Shadow and Freddie's omega mother, Tina Wong.

***

Sebastian

Freddie jumps to his feet.

"Mother." He swallows hard and then adjusts his clothes and pushes his hair back. It's not good if Freddie Fucking Wong is nervous.

All three of us alphas stand at attention.

This is the last thing we need.

"Freddie, how long have you been in the city, and I haven't seen you once?"

Shit, it's starting.

I ran into the woman in the lobby and tried my best to avoid her attention. I was unsuccessful, obviously. She scares the piss out of me. The last time I saw her was in her townhome two years ago. Shadow, Jake, and I were invited to dinner. We'd been a pack for three years at that point. I was very much aware of Shadow's parents' disapproval of our pack. I wasn't aware that they had been planning on keeping Shadow there with them and sending us away with a pile of "fuck off" money and a kick in the pants.

Jake speaks up next, "Tina. It's a pleasure. Would you like a seat?"

She turns to him like a master might turn to his unruly dogs. "Absolutely not. It's uncouth to discuss family matters in public. Freddie, let's go to your suite. Where is my other son?"

Jake turns to me, and my face gets hot.

"I'll go get him."

I turn on the ball of my foot and take off like a bat out of hell. This is just what we need. Mrs. Wong. Her purse probably costs more than the house I grew up in.

I get into the elevator up to the pool and cringe. What on earth are we going to do about Ondine? I don't want her anywhere near Tina Wong. She'll eat her alive.

And I don't care to hear her opinion about my omega.

Is that why she's here? She's heard we have an omega? She's always been way too nosey about our business. Or is she here just for Freddie and his hunt for her husband's would-be killer?

I get to the pool and exit the elevator. It's down a hall and to the right. I check my phone and see an old text from Jake. Ugh. Yes, I've been grumpy feeling Shadow's lust through the bond. When they are together at the house, I'm nearby. I'm working right now, and I can't keep my focus on everything at once.

I use my key card to enter the pool reserved for just the upper-level rooms. It looks empty. But it's hard to see anything with all the trees and shit.

"Shadow? Ondine?" I call out. I hear Ondine make a little noise. Well, at least she's here.

I walk around the path and up a couple of steps, then around the privacy wall. Shadow is nowhere to be seen, but Ondine is in the hot tub. Her upper body is lying on the concrete, while the rest of her is in the still water. She's got her head in her arms.

"Ondine?"

She makes a little noise of acknowledgment, but otherwise remains still.

"What is going on? Where's Shadow?"

I crouch down next to her and put my hand on her head.

"Sweetheart, what's going on?"

She sits back, and I see her face all red and puffy from crying. I pull her towards me, and she steps out of the hot tub, and I get her into my arms.

"I'm fine," she squeaks. She's not fine.

I take her into the locker room and use my nose to find where her things are. She's shaking in my arms, probably from the cold air.

"Hey sweetheart, it's ok. I got you." I rub my hands on her body wherever I can touch, trying to ease her.

"Sabbies?"

The largest smile I've ever felt on my face erupts. She just called me Sabbies. Fuck, that's amazing. A chemical I didn't even know existed pulses in my veins.

"Yeah, I'm here. Let's get you dressed, ok?"

She looks at me with her sad eyes, and my heart aches for her. I don't want her to start crying, at least until she's dressed. I push her swimsuit down, and she steps out of it. I have her step into her underwear and pull them on, as well as her jeans. They are really loose, so I pull off my belt and thread it through her loops. Jake's shirt is folded up neatly in the locker, and I ease her into it, buttoning the middle buttons. I tie the loose ends on the bottom together. I shuck out of my suit jacket and have her wear it over top.

I sit her down on a bench and get her socks and shoes on.

"Sabbies?"

"Yes, sweetie, I'm here."

"Where's Shadow?" she says, barely above a whisper.

"I don't know. I thought he was here. Maybe he's gone back to the suite. We will meet up with him soon."

"He left me. He said...I don't know."

"What did he say?"

She looks like she knows she just doesn't want to talk about it. I give her some time to get the courage.

"He said really nice things. And I thought we were going to...I don't know. He kissed me. But then he used his alpha bark on me, and then left me."

Oh, no. Fucking Shadow. He made the omega cry. I bring her into me, tucking her head under my chin. She relaxes, and I squeeze her tight.

I'm trying really hard not to go hunt Shadow down and lose it. Not just for making her cry. He's not allowed to use his alpha bark on her. Not only is it explicitly against our contract, it's devastating to have it done to you. He's used it on me before, just because I was curious. And it's...frightening.

My phone buzzes. It's Jake.

"Shadow is here. Do you have her? Bring her back to me."

I've never known Jake to be needy. It's kind of endearing.

"Yeah, I got her. We're coming."

He ends the call.

"Come on, sweetheart, let's get out of here."

She's clinging to me, and that's fine with me. I interlace our hands and walk her out.

She's so compliant. She just follows me. She lets me take the lead. Her head is low in submission. I rub little circles on the palm of her hand. We get into the elevator, and I turn to her. She has a single tear track coming down her cheek.

"I'm sorry. I don't know why I'm emotional," she says apprehensively.

Oh fucking hell.

"You can have whatever emotion you want with me."

Why did Shadow leave her like this?

I kiss her forehead.

"Jake needs you. I'm taking you to him. He'll make you feel better." I tip her head up and look over her face. "You're already looking better."

I look over her neck and shoulders. His alpha bark is very powerful, and I can only imagine how easy it was for him to use it on her, and how affected she was, how scary that must have been. His alpha bark is no joke. I pull her closer to me, and we finally make it to the suite. In the vestibule, I can hear arguing. Great, Omega Wong is still here.

I turn to Ondine and fix her hair, wipe her tears, and smile at her. "Chin up, young lady."

She cocks her head to the side, confused at my words. It's something I would tell my sisters before they had to face a hard day. It always worked for them.

I give her an encouraging nod, and then she raises her chin and squares her shoulders. Her breathing is normal, and she looks so much better.

See, it works.

We enter the room, and it's just as you'd expect. Tina Wong sits in a wingback chair facing the living room area, and Shadow and Freddie stand before her, like she's the queen and they are wayward princes. Jake is leaning against a wall nearby. He sees us enter and pops up. He is over to us in just a few strides. He wraps his arms around Ondine and brings her up and in for a hug, ripping her out of my hand.

He mumbles something into her neck.

"Jake," I say. "Jake."

"What?" he mumbles, but then lifts his head to me.

"Shadow used his alpha bark on Ondine," I say as simply as possible. I don't exactly want Queen Tina to hear.

Jake's eyes darken, and he spins towards Shadow while he's still holding Ondine. Freddie, Shadow, and Tina are looking at us. They've stopped arguing.

"What's that?" Tina asks, clearly referring to Ondine.

Jake holds her tighter. "Tina, this is Ondine. Pack Meier's omega."

Silence.

17

Master

Ondine

The woman's stature may be slight, but her aura radiates everywhere, like a radioactive isotope. I assume the reason the room is warm and agitated is from her. I also assume Freddie and Shadow's submissive, mirrored poses are because of this woman. She's impeccably dressed. She's wearing a lilac cashmere sweater and a burgundy cashmere beret on her shiny black hair. She has these high-waisted plaid pants that have a shimmer woven in the material. Her designer black shiny boots are flawless. I can see a stunning plum duster lying across a stool by the kitchen, next to a Hermes handbag.

Standing before her wearing my oversized blue jeans, Jake's button down, and Sabbies's suit jacket—I look like a homeless person who scored big in the last dumpster she was in. I also smell like chlorine. Her nose twitches in disgust. I resist the urge to fix my hair.

I'm in no position to face this powerful omega, the mother of two of the alphas in this room. Shadow. He left me there after professing his feelings for me. I thought...I thought...

I mean, fuck Shadow.

But that kiss felt like one of those pivotal life-changing kisses.

He kissed me like I've never been kissed before, and then he left. I thought something different was happening. But after he left, I realized I was wrong. It wasn't just him telling me he had feelings for me, it was also him telling me he doesn't want to have feelings for me.

'I want you, and I don't like that I want you.'

That's why I didn't go after him. I couldn't decide if it would be fair to ask him to be with me, knowing I might just leave him after all in the end.

He left me first.

I clear my throat. "It's a pleasure to meet you, Mrs. Wong."

My voice, normally soft and small, cracks. I look at Sabbies and point to my throat. He jumps away to get me a bottle of water.

"Ondine, is it?"

"Yes, ma'am."

She waves her hand. "Call me Tina."

"Tina," I repeat to make sure she means it.

Sabbies returns with my water, and I drink the whole thing in one go and then hand him the empty bottle. Jake pushes him, a silent command to get me a second one.

"How long have you been with my son?"

What kind of question is that? I look at Shadow, whose eyes are fixed on the carpet. I then look at Freddie, who is staring holes into my face.

Jake answers for me. "We've had her for a few weeks now."

"Oh, good, so only a little bit. How did you acquire her?"

No one answers her. I certainly won't.

I'm not about to tell this woman I'm a stray omega Jake found on a train with some other man's cum running down my leg.

She pivots to Shadow. "Yin, explain everything now."

Shadow takes a deep breath, "Yes, Mom. It's just new. We'd been considering an omega for various reasons. Jake found her. It was an advantageous decision. Her contract is up after her next heat."

"I'm so confused, Yin. If you were looking for an omega, why didn't you come to me? I have already vetted many wonderful choices for you. And for Freddie."

Shadow stands up straight. "This was a pack decision. It didn't concern you. If I needed your help, I would have gone to you. I'm perfectly aware of the support you can offer."

Tina clicks her tongue. "Yin, I don't want to argue with you tonight. I didn't come here for that. But this is unacceptable. I'm completely thrown. But I don't know why I expected anything less. This is just like when you put in the papers for your pack with Jake."

Why does she hate Jake? Just because he's young and a bit psychotic? Her son is just as eccentric, honestly.

I'm not listening exactly, but I catch the gist of it while they argue: Jake, Shadow, and Sebastian registered as a pack without the Wongs' approval. And they registered with Jake's surname, Meier. Double insult. The Wongs believe their son should be pack leader. He's bigger, older, and has a more important family legacy. Triple insult. And now the pack is trialing an omega that the Wongs have no control over. Quadruple insult.

This poor woman has *never been more insulted*.

My stomach chooses this moment to rumble. Why does this pack always fight before a meal? It's literally the worst timing.

"We have dinner arriving any minute," Jake interrupts the family dispute. "Tina, are you joining us?"

She waves her hand and turns away. It's a yes, I think. Thankfully, there's a ring at the door. Sebastian goes to let in the staff with dinner. It smells amazing. They lay it on the long dining room table and leave.

I am bouncing on my feet in anticipation. I can't even look at anyone. My eyes are zeroed in on the food.

The little cat finally makes an appearance, jumping on the table. I pick her up and sit down, placing her on my lap. She sits down and peeks over the table with her little Batman ears. Jake chuckles at me and comes over. "I'll make you a plate, baby. Just sit tight."

Tina sits at the head of the table, and Freddie takes it upon himself to make her a plate. Once we have our food, the rest of the alphas take theirs. Jake last. He sits at the other head of the table, to my right. The little cat keeps meowing at pretty steady intervals.

Tina says, "So you came with a cat?"

It takes me a second to realize she's talking to me.

"The cat's mine, Mom. Her name is Princess." Freddie says over his food. It's Italian. Pasta with red sauce, pesto, and clam sauce. Garlic bread. Salad with salami and peppers. And some really good soup with kale in it. I give Princess some clams from my pasta, which she gratefully scarfs down. She's polite, though, and doesn't ask for seconds.

Tina mutters something for only Freddie to hear, but we can all guess it's something like, "At least a cat isn't an omega."

God, she is so rude.

Well, I can be rude too. And since I'm temporary, I say, fuck it.

"Where are your alphas, Miss Tina? Do they have a free night tonight?"

She drops her fork. I am so happy I can control my face because I'm absolutely laughing inside. She sighs like she has to explain something to an idiot.

"My alphas," she says tightly, "do not have a *free* night. Yin's father is just finishing work at the courthouse. He'll be by soon. Freddie's father is meeting with some officials here at the hotel."

"Why do you call him Yin?"

She lowers her gaze at me. Oh, I guess only she can ask me questions?

"Because that's his name."

Shadow explains, "Freddie always called me Yin Yin, which sounds like 'shadow' in Mandarin."

He resumes eating and not making eye contact with me.

"Would you let me call you Yin Yin?" I ask, and Shadow chokes on his salad. I guess that's a no.

"You want to call him by his real name and yet you didn't even know it..." Tina says quietly and cruelly.

I'm about to retort something good but devastating, but I don't get the chance because Shadow says, "It's not my real name. Shadow is my real name."

Alphas traditionally change their name when they register in a pack. It's very common for them to legally change their name to a nickname. Like Blaze or Canon or something. Yin was his birth name, but it's no longer his real name.

He's so serious it makes me stop asking questions. But at least it frees my mouth up to start eating. Well, I'm too tired and hungry to be a bitch. I'm conceding. Omegas are hungry things. I need food. And water. And vitamins. Oh shit. One thing I was told hundreds of times by the staff at the Heat Clinic is to take daily multivitamins specifically designed for me.

They prevent my heats from getting too long. And they prevent so many other issues an unbonded omega may have. I haven't had a bond issue since I started taking them.

I've honestly been avoiding them. They taste like crap, and there are so many that they make me swallow. I didn't get them when Sebastian and I went to my place, but I can't go any longer.

I turn to Sabbies and say just to him, "Can you take me to my apartment here soon?"

He stops chewing and looks at Jake. So I look at Jake.

He asks, "Why do you need to go to your apartment?"

I steal a quick glance at Madame Stick-up-her-ass, but she doesn't appear to be paying attention to us. She's talking to Shadow and Freddie.

"I need some things. And also," I lower my voice, "I think the contract is void."

"On what *fucking* grounds?"

"Shadow..." I hiss. Jake waits for me to finish my sentence. I could keep this a secret, but I want to wield this information like a weapon, so I say, "He used his alpha voice on me."

Jake looks at me for three beats. I see it happen like this: he doubts me, then he tries to justify it, and then finally, on the third beat, he gets angry. At first, I think he is angry at me because he's looking me in the eyes, but that isn't the case. He grips his fork tight, turns to Shadow on his left, and flings himself on the man.

Tina screams. Like an old Hollywood scream. Sabbies grabs me and yanks me out of the seat, holding me to his chest, and hits the wall behind us. Freddie grabs his mom and starts guiding her to the door. She rakes her hands over her face in horror.

Oh no, no, no.

Jake straddles Shadow. He's on his side, and his leg on the ground gets pinned by Jake's knee. Jake slams down on his torso, twisting it so Shadow's chest is to the ground. He's contorted and completely trapped. I see the fork sticking out of the back of Shadow's neck, blood oozing out onto the white carpet.

"You violated the contract!" Jake screams into Shadow's ear. "Answer me!" Jake dips down and bites Shadow on his shoulder. This makes both me and Tina scream. Sebastian tightens his arms around me as my knees give out.

It's so violent.

With a mouth full of blood, Jake roars, "I did this for you! I brought her for *you*! And this is what you do with my gift!"

A wave of power falls over everyone in the room, demanding we submit to Jake's authority. Freddie grabs his mother more forcibly and drags her to the door.

"You can't make my mother submit, Jake! Hold back! Pull it back!" Freddie is yelling, but it feels like we are in a wind tunnel, so it's muffled. He manages to get her coat and expensive bag, thrusting them into her arms.

"Let go of my son! Don't kill my son!" Tina screams.

Jake continues to fight Shadow, punching his sides and stomach. Freddie tells his mother, "This is pack business, do not get involved!"

"But he's my son!"

"He's Jake's and you know it."

"Challenge him!" she screams at Shadow, but then turns to Freddie, "Challenge him!"

"I would never do that, and you should never ask me. If Jake feels Shadow needs to be punished, I would not step in," Freddie tells his mother. Jake growls and bares his teeth, but pulls his power back. I gasp at the release.

Freddie finally gets his mother out and into the elevator. She wouldn't have gone if she continued to feel that presence, that power that makes everyone feel like they need to submit or challenge. It's a unique ability only a few pack leads have. Only very strong pack leads.

Freddie returns, and there's a quiet that moves with him. Like the eye of the storm.

"Explain yourself, Shadow. Explain," Jake pants. He presses into the back of his neck with his forearm. He's got his whole body on Shadow's, driving his knee into the soft part of his thigh and chin tipped up and pinned on the carpet.

"We kissed! We kissed, and I didn't want it to go any further. I just needed her to be still."

Jake doesn't react.

"Why?"

"It's too much, Jake. I fall too easily. You know that. And she's so..."

Jake shakes his head back and forth, confused and startled by this information.

Shadow closes his eyes in pain.

Sebastian's hand comes up to my face, and I lean into it. He begins to purr lightly, and it calms me.

"I wasn't thinking. I know we aren't supposed to use it on her. I know," Shadow says.

"I can't believe you fucked up. She can't be treated that way, Shadow. No matter what you're feeling. No matter what."

Jake lifts his forearm off of Shadow's neck. He presses his palm to the bloody bite mark, tenderly, like he doesn't want to see it.

"I'm going to punish you for your crime against an omega, Shadow. Ondine," he looks up at me, "if you ever fucking say you're going back to your apartment again, I'll tie you to my bed for a week. Don't you get it?"

His chest is heaving with anger. I gulp.

"You're not fucking going anywhere. You're staying with us."

Because I'm an idiot, I say, "But I need some things."

"What fucking things?" Jake asks, and Sebastian whispers "Don't" in my ear at the same time.

"My vitamins. My omega vitamins."

Jake closes his eyes in exasperation. "Sabbies can take you to the pharmacy."

"But they are from the Heat Clinic. Special for me. They took a blood test. They have hormones in them."

Sebastian relaxes behind me. He must feel something through the bond. Jake says, "Then we will get you a new doctor to prescribe new ones. What kind of hormones were you taking, baby?"

"Regulators. Since I was with so many different alphas at the Clinic, who weren't mine, I need regulators. And a dose of heat suppressants."

"Well, you don't fucking need that shit anymore. You have us."

I do my very best not to inform him I only have them one more heat. I do a really good job.

"But I can't just go off of them. It's messing with me. I think that's why his bark affected me so much."

Shadow pipes into our tangent argument. "My family has a doctor on retainer. I can have her come to the hotel and draw blood. Get you new vitamins and hormone supplements you need."

Jake turns to his form on the ground. "Look at you, being helpful."

Freddie says, "I'll call her now. She's an alpha. But I'll have her bring her beta assistant."

Jake seems more relaxed having solved a problem. He gets off of Shadow and pulls him up to his feet in one motion, like Shadow weighs absolutely nothing despite being larger than Jake.

He lets him go, and then that blanket of authority comes down again. Shadow bends his head down in submission. But Jake wants more. Sebastian, behind me, also bends his head down.

Shadow dips down lower at his waist.

Jake stands there for what feels like forever.

"That will do for now. Get back to the house. I want you in charge of making room for a nest for Ondine's next heat. I want you back in the city tomorrow."

Shadow replies with "Yes, Alpha," and he leaves without sparing anyone a glance. He doesn't spare anyone a glance. He leaves as quickly as possible with his head still bowed and a fork still sticking out of his skin.

I don't realize I'm shaking until Sebastian rubs my arms. "It's ok," he says in my ear, "It's just adrenaline. It'll go away soon."

Freddie tells us the doctor will be by shortly. Her office is nearby. Jake looks at his knuckles, where the skin has split even more. He looks up and we lock eyes.

"He hurt you."

I'm still shaking. "He just kind of scared me. It felt momentarily...like I'd lost myself. I didn't like it."

He breaks eye contact and turns to Freddie. Freddie is standing by the door with wide eyes and a frown.

"Freddie, I wonder if your mom will think of me differently after tonight? It's funny, she's always implying I'm not strong enough to be pack lead. She's openly said I don't deserve to be in the same pack as Shadow. But I don't think this will do me any favors to win over Tina Wong."

"I don't know, Jake. I've never seen an alpha do that before. You were ready to unbond him, it felt like."

I gasp. Unbond him?

"Relax, sweetheart," Sabbies says in my ear, "We wouldn't reject Shadow. Not unless he didn't submit."

"Or if he doesn't fucking learn from this." Jake takes a napkin from the table and blots the blood off his hands. Then he wads it up and slams it on the table. "That fucker!"

We all just wait. Jake is so high-strung and volatile right now.

"Freddie. I want to go home and deal with my pack. How much longer is this fucking job?"

"I don't know."

"What's the end goal? We found the shooter."

Freddie walks away from the door and down into the sunken living room. He sits down on the couch. "My mother wants him dead."

I must make a noise that indicates my feelings about what he said.

"What, little Ondine? You don't think he should die?"

I shake my head at him.

"Ok, then tomorrow, when everyone is bright-eyed and bushy-tailed we will make a plan. And then me, my pack, and my omega will go home."

Jake continues, "Sabbies, help me clean this up. Ondine, go sit down, baby, you're shaking like a leaf."

Because it's nice to not have to think, I do exactly as he says. I go down where Freddie is and sit down. I sit on the corner, next to him. I tuck in my legs and lean on the armrest. He takes a throw blanket and lays it over me. Out of nowhere, Princess the cat jumps up on me. Making a home on the indent of my waist.

The doctor comes shortly after, and thankfully, I don't have to move. She takes my blood. Her beta nurse hooks me up to an IV and gives me a bag of saline with vitamins and minerals. And he patches Jake's hands.

My prescription will be ready in a few days, she says.

I'm so drowsy by the time it's done, I need to be carried to bed.

18

Kiss Kiss

Ondine

I awake to a little cat attacking my toes from atop the covers. It's been two days now since that awful night. I haven't seen Shadow. I spent nearly all of yesterday in bed. Jake brought me meals. Sebastian brought me clothes from the house. Freddie listened to me play the piano in the late afternoon. I took a bath. Watched movies.

And the men schemed. I don't know what else to call it. For hours, the suite was filled with beta security officers and the alphas (I hid in my room). Apparently, Man-ho is gone. My guess is he got spooked when they jumped his assassin and fucked his secretary.

Last night, Jake asked me not to leave him.

"Shadow used his alpha voice on you without my permission, so you have every right to claim the last of the money and leave us," he said. "But I'm asking you to keep it intact. I can't imagine this being the end."

It's not a bad idea to stay with them one more heat. I'd save money on a heat clinic. And I would get to put off making an appointment at one. I haven't even called to see if I'm banned for life. Or Arnie is trying to find me to press charges.

So, I accepted his request, and then just burrowed in bed another day.

I'll face my problems when I'm Future Ondine.

She always knows what to do.

Or just has all new problems, making the old ones matter less.

My stomach grumbles, and I toss the covers off, sending Princess flying. She darts away when she safely lands on the rug.

I'm wearing one of Jake's t-shirts. It's white and long enough to cover my toosh. I pad along the floor to the kitchen. There's some fresh coffee on the cradle and I'd love to be able to drink some. I look around, and no one is here. I turn on the faucet to the hottest setting and slide over my catnip tea (Sabbies got me tea bags from the restaurant when he picked up my vitamins). I pour the water into the mug, dunk my cute little pyramid tea bag in, and put the mug in the microwave.

"Microwaved tea? Being an omega must be a nightmare." Freddie comes up behind me and leans on the counter. I turn and face him.

"We all must make do when there's no electric kettle."

His snarky little smile falters. "I'll get you one today."

I laugh. "It's fine, Freddie. Maybe you'll find your man today, murder him, and we will all be out of here."

I know I say it casually, but the whole thing is so perverse.

"You hate that I'm going to kill him."

His tone is weird. Like he's being vulnerable.

"I don't know all the details, so I can't judge."

"Tell me."

I sigh. "You told me there's a school of boys being abused. If killing Man-ho saves them, then I understand."

His mouth parts. I don't think he expected me to say that.

"Oh, princess, you truly amaze me."

The microwave dings, and I take my mug out. "Don't call me the same thing you call your cat."

"If I would have known you'd be here, I wouldn't have named her Princess," Freddie says. What does that mean? Is he teasing me? I make a noise like "I don't know what *that* means."

I add some sugar and half and half to my tea.

"Maybe I'll rename her. So far, Sabbies calls her 'Killer', so maybe that's a more fitting name."

I smile at him and sip my tea.

I like it when people call him Sabbies. That's such a cute nickname.

Freddie pushes off the counter and steps closer to me. I can't back up anymore, so I just have to stand there as he gets closer. He dips his head and takes a deep breath through his nose.

"You smell different."

"Do I?" I say softly. Not that there's any other way for me to say things.

Freddie says, "Yeah, you do. You smell *more*. At first, it was just vanilla. Then more of a vanilla ice cream. Now you're like that vanilla ice cream, homemade with too much vanilla bean."

I take a sip of my tea, tasting the catnip pretty strongly. "That's very specific, Freddie."

He grabs my hips, but his hands slide up so he's got a good grip on my torso, and he pops me up off the ground and onto the counter. I squeak in surprise.

"Now you aren't so damned short."

I roll my eyes. He puts his hands on either side of me. "You're fun to have around."

I shrug. "You've never spent time with an omega. Did you know it would affect you so much?"

He winces. "You aren't just any omega, Ondine. You're you. Sure, yes, the alpha side of me is singing. But I also like listening to you play piano like a fiend. Drink your silly tea. Talk to Jake like he's not a homicidal maniac. I like hearing you tap your fingers on every surface in some sort of melody. I like knowing what kind of panties you wear every day. Blue today, princess."

I'm barely breathing.

Freddie shouldn't be saying these things. He's not part of the Meier pack. He's their client. Shadow's brother. An unattached, unbonded alpha.

Is this Boone all over again? Will Sabbies come in and see us and then hide me further away?

I think the only reason this has happened with both Boone and Freddie is that they are so close to the Meier Pack. Any other alpha would smell Jake on me and not take the chance. But Jake makes friends. He holds people in confidence.

And my unwavering loyalty (ha!) aside, this is working on me. I like talking with Freddie. I don't want it to stop. I didn't feel this connection with Boone. Actually, if I'm being honest with myself, I didn't like any of my interactions with Boone.

The heat coming off Freddie's body makes my body relax. I want to curl up into him. I want to kiss the column of his neck. I want his hips pressed into mine. I want him to whisper in my ear all the dirtiest things. I want to interlace our fingers. I want to sit on his face.

I take a sip of my tea.

"You're ridiculous. Jake will kill you. You were there when his own pack mate misbehaved. What do you think he'd do to you?"

Freddie shrugs and gives me one of his stunning smiles. God, this man. I push my legs together to prevent any undue reactions from my sex.

"I have no plans of challenging Jake. He may be a decade younger than me, but I know the order of things. Jake is a good alpha."

He's being genuine.

He's not teasing me to get back at Jake. He's just here, teasing me for fun.

"Make me some cereal, please?" I ask before my stomach growls. His smile grows wider. "Anything, princess."

He leaves me on the counter to get a bowl.

Did I mention he's shirtless? Not sure I did. Perhaps I wanted to keep that detail out of it. But he is. And it's my absolute pleasure to get to stare at his body while he performs a little task for me.

"Can I ask you a question?" Freddie asks me.

"Sure."

"I'm curious about the Heat Clinic. And the alphas they...provide for you."

"Ah."

"Was it difficult not to form a connection with them? Considering they helped you with your heat."

I know he's talking about the alphas, but I can't help but think about Arnie. It was really difficult not to form a godawful crush on the beta who helped me.

"No, not really. We all took blood tests to determine biological compatibility. They were on birth control shots. Which dulls their scent. They were working, so that helped. I would choose three or four during my heat spikes to be with me during my heat. I get really groggy and blank out after knotting, so it didn't really feel like anything at all. It was just...satisfying a need. They were all trained to say and do the same things, so the experience was nearly identical between them."

"So it was different with the Meier Pack."

"That's a personal question," I say, but he's got me thinking. They'd never knotted an omega. They were clumsy and unsure. Excited and inexperienced. And entirely more. More satisfying, even if it could have been better.

It was different with the Meier pack.

Freddie watches me eat my breakfast and cleans up after me. He helps me off the counter, and I leave him with his semi-hard on to go spend the rest of the day in my room.

But what he asked kept with me. I'd never once felt a connection with my previous partners. But just seeing Jake on that train was more powerful than knotting with a Heat Clinic alpha. And being near Freddie? It's more than a crush.

***

Sebastian

I walk into our house on the peninsula, and it's empty like a shell. It's colder than it should be. It's lost a lot of its smells. Jake asked me to check on Shadow's progress with the nest. But this place looks abandoned. Or maybe I am just being dramatic.

Probably. The only time I feel at home lately is with my omega. With Ondine.

I walk through the house, and my footsteps echo. This house has three levels. The main level is where the kitchen, laundry, mud room, piano room, and tv room are. The stairs take me up to the second level with all the bedrooms. Four bedrooms. I stop in front of Ondine's room. It's pretty bare except for some storage stuff from the three of us and the leftovers from her sad little nest.

The next set of stairs is at the other end of the house. Next to Jake's room. They take you up to the lookout. That's my best guess for Ondine's new nest. I honestly think this house was designed for it. The windows are high up, and there are built-in benches. There are skylights. I close the door behind me, and the rest of the house is completely cut off.

Shadow tried. I can say that. There is a nice platform bed. It's round. It has a single blue sheet on it. There are shopping bags piled on the side with, hopefully, the rest of Ondine's nesting materials. She's going to need window coverings. An air filter and ceiling fan. A mini fridge would be good too. But after one day, it's not, not bad. At least all our storage has been moved out.

He's trying.

I hear the front door shut from inside the house. Someone is here. I check my phone, but my agents are with Shadow in the city. Maybe it's Emmerson.

I leave the nest to go find the intruder.

As I walk down the stairs, I hear him in the kitchen, and when I round the corner, I see and smell him at the same time. Boone. He's got his cowboy hat on, only a white undershirt, and his blue jeans hanging off his hips. He peeks his head up from the fridge.

I catch his scent, and there's something off about it. It's usually that outdoor, sunshine smell, but today it smells like the harsh sun on a dry dusty day.

"Howdy, Sabbies, I saw your truck out front," he says and then stands up, shutting the fridge door.

I sigh and sit on a stool by the counter. "What're you doing here?"

"Ah, you know, just making sure you guys have meals whenever you make it home." He smiles at me, and I have to turn my head so I don't stare.

He's so annoying.

Of course, we have meals. I meal prep every month, putting everything in the freezer.

"Wanna go shooting?" he offers.

I wave him away. And then loosen my tie. "I don't have time. I've got to get back. I'm catching the next train out soon. I just came back to check on Shadow's...project."

His eyes reach his hairline. "Project?"

Boone opens the fridge back up and takes out two Cokes, then opens one and slides it to me.

"He's been tasked with getting the nest together. It's a pseudo-punishment for what he did to Ondine."

I drink nearly half the Coke.

"What did he do?" Boone asks in that stupid way of his that makes me want to give him an answer. He's so charming with his rumbly, deep voice.

"He used his alpha voice on her. Made her cry."

I watch his face fall open in shock, but he's got a smile still on, so it looks off. Like he's happy this happened?

"She's fine. I checked on her this morning. It was technically a violation of the contract. But Jake put a stop to that, at least for now. They talked, and she said she wanted to see it through her next heat. Who knows what'll happen next?"

Under his breath, Boone says Shadow is a motherfucker. The two of them have never really gotten along.

I remind myself I have to get back to the city soon. Freddie wants to attend this whiskey tasting at the Fine Bastian Club, a private members-only club downtown. The building looks like what haunted houses look like, even with gargoyles, but it's all legit. Man-ho is a member, just like Senator Wong. They both RSVP'd months ago. Freddie wants to approach him and challenge him. He's very confident he can handle himself. But as his security team, we'll be there for him.

Man-ho is a scary son of a bitch. I wouldn't challenge him unless I was prepared not to make it to tomorrow. Freddie has every right to challenge him after he came after his father.

While I was lost in thought, Boone made his way closer to me. When I open my eyes, he's leaning on the counter next to my stool, looking me in the eye.

"Care to talk about it?"

"No."

He clicks his tongue, which just makes me look at his mouth. My breathing becomes a bit labored, and I look away again.

"Have you been able to spend more time with her? Ever since you yanked her out of here the other day?"

I immediately bite back, "And if I were even ten minutes later, you'd be all over her. Don't deny it, you rake."

He just takes my insult. "A rake? Did you learn your insults from old romance novels?"

Maybe. I do have a lot of sisters.

"Shut up."

"What are you so worried about, my friend?" he asks in his cowboy drawl. "You look burdened."

I make an exaggerated sound, then take a deep breath, then the words come tumbling out, "I feel like I wasted all this time giving her space. I thought she was just here to set Shadow right. Maybe bring our pack some balance. Temporary placements are common enough.

They can be healthy. But things just keep getting more nuts. Jake is losing his mind. He's absolutely crazy for her. Shadow, goddamned Shadow, he's getting worse. And I can't bear the thought of her leaving us after her next heat."

Boone lifts his hand, and I track it the whole way as he brings it closer and closer to my face. I hold my breath, seeing what he's doing. He's going slow enough I could swat him away, but I don't.

He strokes the blade of his finger across my eyebrow and follows it around my ear, and then he tugs my earring playfully. I'm still not breathing.

"You don't think you can convince her to stay with you?"

I think I'm going to pass out.

"I didn't know..." My mouth goes dry.

He smiles at me, and there's genuine affection there. He's so close to me.

"I think I can help you. We can seduce Ondine, together. Didn't we do good by making her feel relaxed when we went to the city? Maybe you should have invited me into her apartment then, so we could show her what two good alphas can do for her."

No, that's not...I want to reject what he's saying, but maybe I should consider it. Is Boone the missing piece? I have to look away from him to try to think straight. If Boone were in our pack, would that make us a better option for Ondine? I can't even piece that together. Especially with him standing so close.

"I thought you turned Jake down," I whisper.

He places his large hand on the side of my face. "You're very handsome. When I first saw you without a shirt, I wanted to lick you from navel to neck. I'm fucking dying to get you naked. No wonder Shadow had a crush on you."

I gasp for air.

What is happening?

He's flirting with me.

"It's a shame you're so slow," Boone says with a teasing smile. "But it's also part of your appeal."

I smack his hand away and stand up.

"Fuck you."

He grabs my torso, and my whole body trills like the keys of a piano. I'm still, but I'm also about to freak out.

"Wow there, we aren't done. I want to help you."

I try to pull away, but his grip on me is tight. He lifts his chin, and he brings us closer. Our heights are the same. Our eyes are level.

"What're you talking about?"

"I can help you with Ondine."

I don't need lessons. I know how to court an omega. I am actually not fucking clueless.

But Boone is confusing me.

And he knows me.

And he's starting to understand Ondine.

I'm suddenly questioning everything I've been doing with her up until this moment.

"What exactly are you offering?"

He smiles, and our noses nearly touch. He loosens his grip on me, but just so he can start this up and down motion on my sides. It's not horrible.

"I've had an omega. Bunny. Remember? So I know how to make her fall in love with you."

I gasp. One of his hands goes between us, and he rakes his knuckles across my abs, over my shirt. It sends shivers all over my body. I remember him talking about Bunny. That was ten years ago, and she passed away. I don't want to ask him what he means. I don't think I can handle hearing more about that tragedy.

Boone looks like he might kiss me. He leans close and everything, but he misses my lips and goes to my ear, where his hot breath adds to the chorus of incredibly confusing feelings. He says in my ear, "Is that what you want? For her to fall in love with you?"

My mouth is hanging open. He moves back to look at me. Our foreheads are nearly touching.

"I want to make her blush," I tell him my secret.

And he knows it's a secret because he doesn't chuckle at me. He doesn't look at me pityingly. He touches my face and brings me to his lips. The kiss is barely there. Because, honestly, I'm scared to death. It's a soft kiss with our slightly puckered lips. Like a first kiss you'd have as a kid.

And it's...confusing.

I'm kissing Boone.

How did I get here? Why was I even in this room? Time no longer makes sense. It's not part of this. My lips are tight, and Boone tries to loosen them with his tongue. But I don't budge. I suddenly become aware of my arms that have been hanging limp at my sides this entire time. I lift my hands to him, but don't do anything with them.

My phone buzzes, and when I open my eyes, time resumes.

It isn't a call, but an alarm.

I'm staring into Boone's possessed brown eyes when I realize I'm going to be late to catch the train.

"Fuck. I have to go."

"Then go," he says, like I'm silly for not realizing. He puts up a finger to stop me, though, and rushes to the counter by the door. He grabs a shopping bag and brings it to me. "For Ondine."

I snatch it from him.

I'm so fucking confused and horny right now. I reach out to the counter to grab my keys, but nothing is there. I twist in circles until I find them in my pocket, then race out of the kitchen.

I run to my truck and hop in. I can make it if I hurry.

A strange feeling of guilt comes over me.

19
Whiskey Tasting

Ondine

T his Whiskey Tasting is more fun than it was pitched to me. It helps that I'm in this mini dress Sabbies brought me. He even gave me shoes. Kitten heels. They are strange, but I'm having a fun time with them.

It also helps that the Wongs are absent.

"Black is your color," Jake says as he scents me for the tenth time tonight. He wouldn't admit it, but he's nervous to have an unbonded omega around so many people. He rubs his neck and face against my throat and jaw over and over. Usually, this act is private, but Jake has decided it needs to be done now.

I'm also, fun fact, a little drunk.

I forgot I have a very low tolerance, or, I've decided, I don't care.

And Jake may be a little drunk, too.

So, when his hand slides up my thigh, exposing my panties, I have to slap him away. He growls at me. I make eye contact with him and say, "You want everyone in this room to see my bare ass? I'm wearing a thong, Alpha Meier."

I'm not sure I get all these words out exactly because he gives me a big Cheshire Cat smile. "Yes. Then I'll have to kill them for it. And that'll be just as fun."

I roll my eyes and turn away from his mischievous, irresistible face. He's joking. He just wants to sound like a baddie. This place is classy as fuck. And intimate. The staff smile at you. All the members of the club know the staff by name. The bartender knows everyone's drinks. The furniture is all old and beautiful and unique. The chandeliers are breathtaking, but I'm the only one looking at them. My pack is so comfortable here. Oh fuck. I mean, the Meier pack.

There are all these tables everywhere with different bottles of whiskey. Everyone brought a bottle. Jake brought something from Japan, and Sabbies brought something from Ireland. I don't know where Shadow is. And there are tiny crystal stemware glasses that you use to taste. So far, I've liked none of the whiskeys. But, I enjoy the tiny cups. Everyone seems to be congregating in the hall, which is the large area at the top of the stairs before you go into the tasting room. And it's where the bar is set up.

Jake toys with my hair. I put it in a half-up, half-down thing with a bow in the back. He likes the front pieces.

"I'm so surprised how quickly you forgave me," he muses with his cute, drunk voice.

"What're you talking about?"

"After what Shadow did to you."

I frown in confusion. He has this strange, vulnerable look to him. Oh, I get it. He thought I would blame him.

Since he's the pack leader, and his pack mate messed up.

I honestly forgot entirely that Shadow messed up. I've mostly been sad that he's been avoiding me. I don't want to think about it too much. I'm feeling too good. So I just lean over and kiss him on the cheek. That does the trick.

He's so simple.

I'm hungry. I try to walk away from Jake, but he snakes his hand around my waist and yanks me into him. This is a fairly casual event, and we shouldn't be this drunk. I don't think. A man near us laughs at the look on my face. He comes over to us. "Jake Meier, who do we have here?"

The man is an omega. How very rare to meet a male omega. I smile really big at him. Thankfully, there are de-scenters in the air conditioning, so I can't scent anyone if they happen to be perfuming. But I can tell all the same.

"My sweet and wicked omega, Ondine. Ondine, meet Geoffrey. His pack is somewhere. Who knows? He was a client of mine while they were courting."

Geoffrey and Jake exchange a handshake hug thing. Then Jake comes back to holding me around my waist.

"You needed security while you were courting?" I ask with wide eyes.

He laughs, and it sounds like pretty bells. Gosh, he's pretty. "I was being courted by several packs. They all had boundary issues, so yes." He laughs like he's remembering something truly outlandish. "I needed round-the-clock security. I think you guys ended up stopping many home invasions, prevented inappropriate gifts from getting to me, and retrieved me from at least two kidnappings."

God, I forgot how heinous alphas are. I hear about this stuff in the news, but not knowing too many omegas, I haven't heard about it firsthand.

Jake beams at Geoffrey. "Oh, we did more than you could imagine. But it all worked out. You were bonded by your next heat. And that was years ago. How's the Aries pack?"

Geoffrey gets stars in his eyes, and he exhales. "I think I hit the jackpot." He addresses me to explain. "I'm bonded with a pack that has two female alphas and two male betas. I know it's strange, but it works so well for us. I think every pack needs a beta. I've never felt more cared for and safe. How are things with the Meier pack, Ondine?"

Betas. Two of them. I can't help but think of Arnie. I wonder where he is. If he ever thinks of me.

Jake isn't worried at all about my answer, but he should be because I'm drunk. "I'm just on a temporary contract. Maybe I'll have to find a pack more like yours with some diversity. Three aggressive male alphas are a lot for one girl. Perhaps I'll get my own security team, too."

Jake slams his whiskey glass on a nearby table and turns to me to see if I'm serious. The flaming anger in his eyes causes my smile to drop. Fuck.

"Excuse us, Geoffrey." Geoffrey has the audacity to smile at me like he knows I'm in trouble. I do not resist the urge to stick my tongue out at him.

Jake pushes the small of my back, leading me to the giant set of stairs and down them. We get to the bottom, and he herds me off to the left. There are these large portraits everywhere of the scariest moth-erfuckers you've ever seen. A male omega named Orrin Cash found the city, oddly enough, and he had a team of alphas that operated outside the law. They weren't his pack. They were actually more like security. They founded this club. Basically, hired killers. Wait. Just like the Meier Protection Group.

He takes me to a small gallery off of some hallway. We enter, and he shuts the double doors, locking us in. There are benches and chairs facing the art on the walls, and some busts in the middle on plinths, running down the center.

"Ondine," Jake growls at me. A warning.

"What?" I say, like I don't know what he's mad at. He paces between the plinths and benches, trying to decide what to say next. I take this break to look at the art. More portraits of scary as shit alphas. Long beards, psychotic eyes, shallow faces. This one reminds me of Shadow. He's got long, black hair and looks just as haunted as my alpha.

"Ondine," he turns to me and gets my attention. "You haven't forgiven me."

I shake my head and say, "It's not that."

"What does that mean?"

Jake is, as always, on the edge of losing it when he's being himself. And he's not holding back with me right now.

I turn to face him. He's on the other side of the room. "I really wasn't too upset about what Shadow did. I was mostly sad he left me alone." I pause to see if he wants to hear more. He doesn't say anything, so I go on. "He led me through it, safely, when he used his alpha bark, and released me quickly. It's honestly not as big of a deal as you all make it out to be. I agreed to carry on with the contract."

He huffs a few times before asking, "Then why are you saying you're going to leave me?"

"You've made me no promises. The only thing we've agreed to is two heats," I remind him. "And it's not like I've proven myself to be this good omega who can help regulate your pack or do anything good for you all. I don't bring much to the table."

"What? You feel like you..."

I cut him off—"Jake, I'm a bad omega."

"What?" He sounds genuinely confused.

"Come on. I'm a bad omega. I was a halfway decent beta. But I'm fucking awful."

"Who told you that?"

I huff out a breath, shocked by his question. No one told me that. At least, I don't think.

"It's true. I didn't enroll in the Institute. I lived on my own. I worked gig jobs. What omega does that? All my alpha partners have been paid for! That shouldn't even be a thing. I don't know how to care for anyone. You brought me here to fix Shadow. And he hasn't even talked to me in days. No one even comes to me for comfort. When I was at your house, I slept alone at night."

His mouth hangs a bit open. He's speechless.

Jake comes right at me and grips the back of my neck. "Have you been doing this the whole time?"

"Doing what?" I rock back on my heels, but he holds me in place with his firm grip.

He grumbles until real words come out. "Not telling me when we do something wrong. Not telling me how to fix it. And just using it to torture yourself."

He didn't do anything wrong. It's all me that's wrong. I don't answer him. His other hand grips my side. He's holding me so tight, and I can tell he'd like to throttle me.

"Why does everyone around me do this!" He doesn't raise his voice, but it's like he's yelling. "Shadow withers away in front of me! And now you! Am I not capable of listening? Do I not make you believe I can solve your problems? Have you not felt my power?!"

"But why even bother solving my problems?!" I shout at him. "I'm a bad..."

"Don't you dare finish that sentence, Ondine. Shut the fuck up. So, what if you didn't enroll at the Institute? It's not required for all omegas. And not all alphas sign up either. It's another government funded bullshit place. Why would I tell you that you should have done anything at all different when I found you as you were? And you worked for yourself? Lived alone? And you stayed safe. And happy. You are a good omega."

The omega in me preens. She believes him. She loves this. She loves being talked to like this. I melt into his touch.

"And we are just learning how to lean on you, too, you know. Maybe we are just as bad alphas. We've been together this long without someone like you. We are learning. We need time. We need more than two heats." His face softens, and he is so close we share a breath. "What do you want? And I will provide."

Kiss me. I think. It's what I want. I'm still feeling good from the alcohol. I want to make out. I want to get another cocktail. I want to talk to more interesting people. The omega in me just wants to fuck, honestly.

We can talk about our difficulties another time.

But I can't get the words out. I don't want to regret them later. I don't know what the right thing is to say.

"Ondine, my dear, I want you." His grip loosens, and he gently strokes my neck with the back of his fingers. "I want you for me. I want you in this pack. You don't have to accept Sabbies or Shadow just yet. I'm your alpha. Your only alpha. I want to be. I've never wanted someone more. I'll give you all the money in the world for your haircuts. I'll protect you from everyone. I'll make sure there's a piano in every room you're in. If you don't ever tell me how to make it right, I'll still try."

Is he proposing that I stay in his pack?

"You're drunk."

"Maybe a little," he admits. "But I'm serious. We can make another contract. A courting proposal. You'll stay in my house. And when you're ready, you'll bond with us. I can take good care of you. I'll show you. We can learn how to be good together."

He kisses my forehead and wraps me up in a hug. He makes me feel so good. Do you accept something like this just because they make you feel good? The omega in me is doing somersaults and saying yes!

I know I want this, but I can't just keep being agreeable and say yes to everything. I have to be sober and actually think this through.

He doesn't expect an answer, and that alone makes me want to accept right now.

He eventually asks, "Do you want an orgasm before we go back?"

I laugh in his arms, and he joins me. "That would be nice, Alpha."

For the first time, I feel his chest rumble with a genuine alpha purr. It is there to be comforting, but right now it's happening because he's so happy.

"You don't deserve an orgasm, you wicked omega." His hands start to pet me up and down my dress. "Every time you say you're going to leave me, I'm going to spank you." Before Jake finishes his sentence, his hand cracks on my ass. It fucking hurts! Fuck! But as the pain dissipates, I'm left a little excited. "Every time you remind me you're on a temporary contract, I'm going to pinch your fucking nipples." I try to leap away, but he has me pinned in his arms, so his thumb and forefinger get my nipple good. I cry out, but it's all pleasure. "And if you ever, ever, talk about bonding another pack, I'll bite you." His mouth is on me so fast I don't even have a chance to blink. He bends my body back and presses his teeth to my collarbone. He doesn't break the skin, but his bite is still rough and hard. I moan, loud and lewd for the act.

A flicker of something passes through us. Like dialing through the radio and signal hits for just a moment, strong and clear. It feels like a bright light. Incredible.

His hand is under my dress before I even know it. My leg lifts up, and he pushes his two fingers into me. I drop my head back, and he bends me even further. His fingers fuck me exactly as I was hoping. I cry out, and he continues to bite my collarbone.

"Jake, fuck. I like this. I like this a lot."

I can feel his smile on my skin. "Good girl. Good fucking omega. Tell me what you like, and you will get everything."

He continues to bend me back until I feel the bench under my back. I lay down all the way, and he kneels in front of me, pushing my dress up to my stomach. He fiddles with his pants until his dick is out. "I'm going to fuck you now."

I assumed as much.

20

The Scent Test

Ondine

We make it back up to the party without anyone saying a damned word about our very lewd exit. My hair is all sexed up, my bow is missing, and Jake's tie is undone. The bartender gives me a knowing look as he hands me my French 75. I wink at him and see Geoffrey nearby, who raises his glass to me. Thank god for the de-scenters, otherwise everyone in this room would smell Jake's cum on me. And my continued arousal.

I toast Geoffrey back with my glass in hand. A man next to him turns him away and squeezes his butt.

Jake asked me to be *with* him. Make him my alpha. Of course, I'm preening. And I'm considering it. He has everything that satisfies my omega side. He's so strong and powerful. He protects me and stands up for me. He's focused on me. He fucks me as much as I need. He says I don't have to be with his other pack mates.

It, honestly, isn't a bad idea.

And he's so handsome, like a movie star. I drain my drink and turn around for another one. I haven't even left the bar. Jake has though. Sabbies came up from downstairs with a security issue. I guess he's been with the valet this whole time. He caught my eye, but just stared at my dress like he'd never seen anything sexier. I didn't mind. He and Jake went downstairs to the front to do whatever they do.

Jake said, on his way out, that Shadow has "eyes on you." And then tilted his head to the corner of the room. So, I guess Shadow is here.

A man sidles up to me, but leaves an appropriate distance between us. He's older. His neck is ungodly in size. He's got a goatee. He's Chinese. He smiles at me, and I give him a half-effort smile back. "You like sparkling wine?"

"Champagne," I correct, and take a sip.

"But California has good options."

I look around to see if someone else notices this strange man next to me.

"Ok."

I turn away, but he just moves to be back in front of me. "My name is Lee. It's nice to meet you."

I blow out all my breath and then give him my attention.

"Hi Lee. I'm Ondine. Are you enjoying the whiskey? Which one did you bring?"

Lee doesn't have anything in his hands. They are in his pockets. "Well, Ondine. I'm not here for the whiskey."

Wow. I do not care for this weird ass conversation. My head is spinning. I don't have Jake with me. I think I need something to eat. In the main room, there are cheese platters.

"Well, ok. Um, have fun or whatever. I'll see you around." I don't wait for his reply before I step away, on my way to cheese. He grabs my arm. Hard.

"*Don't walk away from me.*" His words are laced with alpha bark. I grit my teeth. Fear and anger rip through me, sobering me up. Who the fuck does this man think he is? Just because an alpha can control an omega doesn't mean they ever fucking should. And for what? So I can have a stupid ass conversation?

I dart my eyes to the corner of the room Jake referenced earlier, and there stands Shadow. He's talking with Freddie. They both have their heads bowed toward each other and very aggressively talking. They don't look at me.

I turn to my assailant. "Fuck all the way off."

"Awe, it's like a kitten spitting at a wolf."

God, this guy is weird.

Someone with a headset on the other end of the room addresses the party. "Everyone, we are about ready to have our blind taste test contest. If you're participating, come see me."

It's enough of a distraction. Lee yanks on my arm and pulls me off through a doorway into a small hall, lined with offices. He practically lifts me off my feet to take me to the end and down some stairs. It's the staff offices. I'm honestly a little curious what the fuck is going on, so I'm not screaming, but I am getting really fucking pissed off.

He pulls me into a room and shuts the door. Thank god we didn't go outside. We are in some sort of classroom thing. There's a board and boardroom style table with chairs. There are men here. Lots of men. All alphas. They are all giving me intense stares.

"Ondine, sit down." Lee throws me into a chair at the head of the table.

"She smells..." one alpha says and slaps his hand over his face. Well, fuck you too.

"Yes," Lee says, "Jake Meier fucked her in the gallery ten minutes ago. It wasn't my plan to bring her in here smelling like him, but you are all just going to have to keep it together."

Guess there are no de-scenters in this room. Tragic because all these male pheromones are egregious.

"Why did you bring me in here? Who are you people?" I ask, and some alphas gasp.

"Her voice!"

Fuck me. Yes, I have a sweet voice.

"Are we going to have a problem?" Lee asks.

"You brought an omega into a room with feral, unbonded alphas. Probably."

My eyes go wide as moons. I'm in danger. Why did it take me this fucking long to realize that?

Oh, I don't want to be here.

And I'm definitely still drunk.

"I'm so glad you all understand what's happening here."

I raise my hand.

Lee looks at me with no humor.

I lower my hand and say, "I don't understand what's happening here."

"We're here, sweet Ondine, to find your scent match. My alphas have been denied access to the Institute. They've been denied omega placement. Their registration for omega Heat Clinics has also been denied. All by Senator Wong. Not one former student of the Man-ho School has been granted placement status at the Cash City Institute. Now, do you find that fair, sweet Ondine?"

This is when my brain catches up. Lee. This man is Lee Man-ho. And these are some of his former students. Or whatever. His men. I don't know how I factor into any of this or why I'm here.

"You're all feral?" I ask before I can stop myself. A feral alpha is basically an animal. It means he can lose his mind and become his base self. Violent, possessive, and driven by his need to feed, fuck, and destroy. They are always teetering on the edge of complete darkness.

"Don't act surprised. You've been around Freddie. He's feral. Are you afraid of him?"

Freddie is. I knew that. That's why he's at the monastery. His chain, I think of. His chain is silver. It keeps him from beasting the fuck out. He's teasing me. And messed with me. But he's never done anything to worry me.

But a room full of feral alphas is different.

"What am I doing here? What does this have to do with scent matches?"

A scent-match is a rare thing. Practically a myth. An omega and a pack of alphas can scent match. It makes them uniquely paired. It's like fate or magic. Scent matches are a supreme match. Like a soulmate.

I actually don't fully understand it.

"It's our workaround. I've found two of my former students' scent matches. I intend to find them all."

There are maybe twelve men in this room besides Man-ho. They all look at me with such craving hope. "So, I'm not being kidnapped?"

Man-ho laughs. Like I'm being silly. "No, not yet anyway. We were all up in the tasting room, but the club has scent blockers. I needed you in here to properly test."

"Why me?"

"To piss off the Wongs, mostly. A scent match would supersede any contract you currently have with them."

I mutter under my breath, "I don't have a fucking contract with the Wongs." My contract is with Jake Meier and his pack.

Man-ho pulls my chair into a more open space in the room and asks each of his men to take a turn, leaning into my neck and smelling me. They all say something about Jake's scent all over me. Which Man-ho barks out why it shouldn't matter. And if they were a scent match, it would make them so insane their feral side would rip out of them, and they'd rush to go kill Jake right now. He says something more graphic about how they'd rip his head off his shoulders, which makes me growl in my pitiful, sweet voice. I get a couple "awes" for that.

I groan in agitation as each man places his hands on the armrests of my chair and leans their head in. Their breath puffs around my ear. It makes it so I have to smell each one. I'm upset when some of them smell kind of nice.

"How do you know we are a scent match?" I ask Man-ho just to break up the silence.

"Sometimes it's obvious. Other times, not as much."

This guy is a really bad communicator. How is it that he has a school?

"What do you mean?"

"Scent matches can be individual. Or they can be for a pack. If the pack is a scent match, it's the pack lead that notices first. Once the omega is bonded, the match is more obvious to everyone. But that doesn't mean the unbonded alphas don't have some sort of reaction. It's an abnormal reaction. Like they can scent you more with more depth. They can feel a cord, as if tied from their heart to yours. They become unnaturally possessive or jealous."

Sounds like hocus pocus to me. Honestly. Another male smells, but this time he rubs his nose across my cheek. Absolutely not. I shove him away, and he laughs. This is gross.

"I've been training alphas to harness their inner beast, give in to the goodness of their wild side, and take their feral natures to the ends of it—but they need an omega. All alphas do. To deny my sons an omega is cruel. It's unnatural. And I will stop at nothing to put a bullet through Senator Wong's head and end his policies."

Ok, so glad I asked. I'm trapped in a room with a would-be murderer. I mean, I suppose I already knew he was pure evil, considering the child abuse Freddie told me about. Had he hurt all these men when they were younger, too? Is that why they're feral? Or why they could never tame their feral side?

But this will be over soon. The last of the men have finished assaulting me with their proximity and breath.

The men surround the table, standing behind the chairs. They chat to each other about my scent. Everyone's a little unsure if we are scent matches, and scarily, everyone is trying to say that they could be. "I don't know, but it is really nice, so she could be. Her voice and that scent?" I start to shift in my seat, realizing the problem here.

Any of these men can just *say* I'm a scent match. Most alphas are already possessive, jealous. Hell, Man-ho's definition could prove Jake has a scent match with me. It's too vague.

I'm panicking.

"Lee, I have a question."

"Yes."

"Who's to say we are matched? Me or...anyone?"

I turn in my chair until I see Man-ho, and he's looking at me like a goddamned predator. Oh, no. I'm in danger. He turns his head, like a doll would, to his men.

"*Do not move!*" He alpha-barks, and his influence rushes out of him like a flash flood. Jake's influence had descended like a heavy blanket, but Man-ho's crashed into us with pure devastation. I've never felt anything like it before. Man-ho's command was for his men, but it sends my omega body into pure submission.

He yanks me out of my chair and throws me headfirst onto the table. I emit a sound to try to calm him, like a purr and whimper combined, and it's totally involuntary. My legs are dangling off the edge of the table. His hand is holding me down by the back of my neck. He goes still. I push the sound coming from my chest louder.

He grips my neck and uses it to yank me back up to standing.

The men haven't moved an inch. Like they are frozen. Even their expressions are neutral. They won't help me.

Man-ho pulls a knife out of his pocket, and it slides open. He presses it to my clavicle.

He drops the hand on my neck, but immediately grabs my torso and pulls me close to him. He's so rough, and I know I'll bruise.

"If you truly think any of you are scent-matches, then try to overcome my alpha influence to save your mate—because if you don't, I will slice her ear to ear and we can hear her pretty little voice one last time."

No one even makes a noise. Man-ho's influence hardens in the room, making it feel like we are getting strapped in.

He twists me so my neck is bare to him. I whimper for my life. "What if I bite her? Would that spur you to act?"

That's it. I'm screaming. I'm screaming so damned loud. But I'm not. Nothing is coming out. "That's a good girl. Stay quiet."

He scrapes his teeth along my neck.

I desperately seek out help from each of the other men. No one has moved, still. No one even looks like they are trying. I'm trying, though. I'm pushing and pushing and pushing.

When will this end? If one of these guys successfully breaks Man-ho's hold? I immediately know I don't want that. That would mean I'm gone. This man would take me away from the Meier Pack. I don't want a single one of these feral fuckers to take me. So where does that leave me?

I want to just wait for Jake to find me. He's got to be looking. I was snatched from him not too long ago. Freddie and Shadow were right there. Sabbies and Jake were one level down (so it's got to be this same level I'm on? Or am I in the basement level now?) I haven't left the building. It can't be that big.

Instead of biting me, Man-ho licks up the side of my face. Gross.

"Aren't omegas just the most adorable things? Can you all hear the noise coming from her chest? She's trying her best to calm me down. But what her body doesn't realize is that I'm already very calm. You know, for the longest time, I believed omegas were utterly useless. Their only purpose was to make alpha babies. They are barely human, you know? Their physiology and personalities are all designed to pro-create with alphas to produce more alphas. But I've since learned they have many uses beyond fucking. Like this noise she makes. Fascinat-ing. Also, their nesting is not completely useless. An alpha can use time in their omega's nest to heal any number of things: depression, old wounds, and hone their minds to solve problems. An omega's fragility is also something to marvel at. The most powerful predator in the world procreates with something so small and soft. You'd think their kids wouldn't be as strong. But alpha chromosomes don't adopt traits associated with their omega parent's size. But what it does take is their intense need to perpetuate the species.

"It's too bad she's so weak. Too weak to ever be considered an equal. Too pretty and sweet to stand next to an alpha and be respected. Too soft and lovely..."

Man-ho pets my body with the knife in his hand. Over my breasts and across my belly and hips. This mother fucker better not be getting turned on.

I cannot listen to any more of his pontificating. It's grating on my ears. He's acting like he's the first idiot who's said out loud that omegas are weak, useless sex dolls. Like he's so damned profound. I get it—it is so difficult to imagine the girl who goes into heat every six weeks and requires men to shoot their cum in her mouth and knot her pussy might be worthy of respect. I'm not even a whole person. I can barely hold a job. I can't live on my own. And then, on top of that, one of these alpha-designated assholes can casually use his alpha bark on me, and I become their slave.

And yet I'm in here, inside of me, and I feel like a real person. I don't feel like I'm any different from anyone. Do I not bleed when cut? Do I not cry when hurt? Do I not hunger and thirst and war with my own nature? Do I not have ambition and love, and hate? I can hate just as well as anyone. I see you just as you see others. Alphas think they are more than everyone. They are more cunning and violent, and powerful.

Yet I see how fucking useless *they* are.

I've experienced it firsthand.

Their alpha bark has no value because they've never fucking used it for anything other than benign oppression. What is it for if not to render their victim quiet enough to take their violence?

An alpha can become feral, which means they are dangerous to everyone around them. At worst, an omega will get bond-sickness—which basically means she could die of a broken heart. We take everything and bury it inside our bodies, keeping it away from the world. While an alpha inflicts all his insecurities and pain onto everyone around them.

Sorry, I'm a soft and sweet, and lovely sex doll. At least I'm not an unhinged nightmare person.

The more I think about how little and small and useless alphas are, the less I feel Man-ho's influence on me. It's like it's running away down a drain. But as I look around, they are still being held by his power. But not me.

I'm not sure why his influence is sliding away from me. Perhaps he thinks he doesn't need to hold me in it anymore. That I've proven my agreeableness.

When I was younger, I took a self-defense course. They taught me how to get out of a hold just like this. I don't remember all the mechanics, but I remember one. You don't lift your leg to then kick back. Your assailant will see you doing it and move out of the way. You have to just kick back from a standing position. I close my eyes and try to imagine exactly where his crotch is in relation to my hip. I'm going to use my hip as a hinge.

He's still talking. Talking about how he's realized omegas have worth because we serve him in so many ways. I wiggle my toes to test my ability to move my body at will. I'm completely out of his influence now.

His crotch is too high up. There's no way I can kick his nuts. What else is full of nerve endings and within my reach?

"Furthermore, they are nice to look at...aghurgh."

The heel of my shoe slams into the bone of his shin, and I continue to scrape it down as hard as I can all the way to his foot.

He releases me so he can use his hands to flail about. I ball up my fist around my thumb and spin around to punch him in the middle of his face. Pain like no other radiates from my fist to my elbow. I cry out in agony. I think I broke something.

All I can think is "out, out, out," so I run out of the room. I remember how we got here, so I just retrace my steps as fast as humanly possible. I'm not even sure my eyes are open because my hand is in so much pain.

21

The Chase

Sebastian

Shadow has completely lost the plot. He pulled out a damned machete out of thin air (I assume) and ran out the front doors after the convoy of black SUVs that pulled out of the driveway moments ago.

I'd called Jake down here when Man-ho arrived. Well, I didn't see him, but his four SUVs pulled up and Cynthia exited wearing a red qipao dress. Her blonde hair was wrapped up with sticks. She was asking for parking passes for all the vehicles. The lot for the club doesn't allow individual club members more than one spot, so the club valet was arguing with the drivers.

I called Jake down to deal with this. Also, so he could see for himself that Man-ho was, in fact, coming.

I didn't expect the jolt of fear and trepidation to come through the bond from Shadow, and then, moments later, the SUVs peel out of the driveway into the street, leaving a frantic Cynthia.

"Where did Shadow get a machete?" Freddie asks next to me.

"I don't know. Why did he take off after them like that?" I gesture down the darkened road.

Cynthia rushes over to Freddie and tries to fling her arms around him, but he bends backwards and stops her.

"Freddie! Oh my god!" His face is all screwed, and he keeps taking steps away from her.

He ends up hiding behind me to avoid her.

Jake rolls his eyes at the woman and says to me, "I'm going to go to Ondine upstairs. You'll have your guys follow Man-ho, see where they ran off to so fast."

I go to answer him, but Cynthia cuts in. "Ondine isn't in there, Jake. She's left with Mr. Man-ho."

Freddie, Jake, and I give her all our attention. She has the audacity to preen under it. She does a little pose, like we are looking at her outfit.

"What the fuck did you just say?"

"They weren't supposed to leave me here. But yeah, they came to talk to the omega and bring her back to the school. I have it all set up for them."

Maybe I'm losing my hearing, but did Cynthia just admit to a plot to kidnap my omega?

"Setup for what?" Freddie asks, because Jake and I are speechless. Freddie sounds angry. Good. I'm glad we are all angry.

"For the scent test. Mr. Man-ho wants to do another scent test. He's found two other scent matches for his alumnus. Can you believe it?! I would sooner eat my own foot than be scent matched to an omega. But they've formed a pack and everything now. I told him about your unbonded, sleazy little omega, and he was very sure he'd be able to do it again."

Jake sweeps his foot against the ground, causing Cynthia to fall right on her ass, and then he turns to me. "How far away is the school?"

Cynthia is crying on the ground, but I think she's fine. There are no actual tears, just crying noises. "Miles. You need a vehicle. Or take the train."

"If I run?"

"30 minutes." He looks like he's going to bolt, so I grab his arm. "Jake, Shadow is running now. He's right on them. He'll get there first." My brain finally catches up with my racing thoughts. "I have men there already. I'll tell them not to let those vehicles get into the campus, ok?"

I get on my open radio channel and tell my men waiting outside of the school all we know. I also berate them for not telling me four fucking SUVs left the school an hour ago. They claim only one did. So I'm assuming the other vehicles came from other locations.

Jake bends down and pulls the crying Cynthia up on her insanely tall heels.

"You're coming with me." Valet heard everything, so they threw Jake a set of keys to a fleet vehicle that was already parked there. Jake throws Cynthia in the back of the van, slides the door closed, and then hops in.

Freddie and I are left. He stands and listens to me on the radio channels with my various teams. He's awfully close to me. I can smell him. Freddie is like that strong black tea smell: citrus, bergamot, and orange. It's honestly potent as hell. I have to breathe through my mouth.

I'm trying to remember smelling him before this, at all. And no, he's been scentless.

He asks, "The vehicles came from other locations?"

"Yeah, from his house. His restaurant. School. And I can't track the last one."

He pops a pill and swallows it dry.

"And all we have to go on is Cynthia's word that they are headed to the school."

I nod and try to step away from him, but he matches me. A breeze comes down between the buildings, and I smell him again. I wonder if Ondine has smelled him. Did she like it? She smells like vanilla ice cream. Would that compete with Freddie, or smell nice together? I breathe in deeply and consider.

I shake my head.

What the fuck am I thinking about right now?

"You don't seem to be worried."

I cock my head to the side and make eye contact with Freddie. "I'm freaking the fuck out, Freddie. But I'm also thinking."

"Tell me."

In lieu of telling him he smells insanely good, I tell him what's also brewing in my head.

"I don't know if I trust Cynthia. I'm sure she is telling the truth, but they left her here. Why did they leave her here?"

We stare at each other. I turn back to the club. "Jake left Ondine upstairs. Shadow was watching her. You were with him. What did you see?"

Freddie shakes his head. "She was standing by the bar. Shadow and I were talking. He was being a little shit, as always. He told me I couldn't go talk to her, but wouldn't go talk to her himself. Next thing we know, she's not there. Shadow looked out the window and saw the cars and ran out of the building."

"How did they get Ondine from the bar upstairs to the cars down where I was?"

He smiles at me. "That's the question. Let's go upstairs and figure it out."

On the way, I get responses back from my teams. All four SUVs have gone in different directions. I tell them to keep on them. Do not lose them. They know this. We all know this. But I don't have anything else to go on.

I grab a staff member, Jessie, and tell her the situation. She looks horrified. "Someone took her from upstairs. Freddie last saw her here." We arrive at the spot by the bar. It's one of those roll away carts they bring out for parties. Freddie starts sniffing around, but he won't smell a thing. The de-scenters here are expensive and thorough. There are a couple of doors nearby. One is a false door that can open the room up to another annex. We searched it completely. The other door leads to the prep area. The main kitchen is in the restaurant on the main level. Before we head down the elevator to the prep area, we check the last door. It leads down to the hallway offices.

"So she had to be taken down through the restaurant kitchen. It's the only way to get outside." I say to Freddie. He agrees, but we both look unsure.

I stop and put my hands on my hips. I'm panicked. That's for sure. I keep thinking about what Man-ho will do with her. He's not going to hurt her. That would be insane. She's an omega. But my greatest fear? That's her finding her scent match.

I rub my chest and, for some reason, say "oww". Freddie grabs my wrist and pulls my hand away from my chest. "Stop that. Unless he took her through the front entrance, the restaurant kitchen only opens up to the back. There's no way they could have gotten her out through here."

I sigh and suggest we go back up and start again. Jake is on their tail. Shadow, wielding a mystery machete, is also on it. I have three different security teams tracking the vehicles. All that's left is where she was last seen.

By the time we get up there, Jessie has got everyone to leave. All that's left is the staff.

"Freddie, you go explore the property. I need to stay here where she was last seen. Until we get eyes on her, we have to cover our bases."

"You got it, boss," he says, but stays right next to me. And he lights a cigarette. The party has cleared. The staff is cleaning. I realized he was being sarcastic when his arm brushes mine.

"Why are you still standing here?"

Freddie gives me his classic punk-ass half smile. "Don't you work for me, Sebastian Meier? Second off," I don't remember a *first off*, "I agree it's a good idea to be here until we know for sure where she is. What is Jake saying?"

The app on my phone I use to move radio channels from my different teams, also has the line for Jake. But I call him instead. He's pissed. Only one vehicle made it to the school. It only has the driver. Shadow took his machete to the whole thing. So that's fun.

Cynthia snuck off and closed the gate.

"Jake, I'm freaking out. What if...what if..." I'm about ready to say the stupid thing out loud.

"What if she finds her scent-match?" Oh, thank god. Jake said it first.

"No, I mean, what if they hurt her?"

"They won't fucking hurt her. If an alpha hurts an omega, the consequences are insane. Not just legally. They could turn feral." God, I don't even want to think about that. They won't even get a chance to go to court. We'd take care of it ourselves.

I resist the urge to rub my chest again. And why the fuck is Freddie standing so damned close to me?!

I nudge him with my elbow and step away, but he just follows me. Then he mutters something about the "fucking de-scenters" before taking a long drag on his cigarette. Which doesn't make any sense for him to be mad about because his cigarette is only allowed because of the state-of-the-art filtration system and de-scenters.

Jessie walks up to us to give me a report on the building. She says that all the guests have been asked to leave, but a lot of them are waiting on valets to get their cars. There are also members in the restaurant. She apologizes and asks if we should call the police.

"Jessie, is there any access from this spot to out front with the valets? Besides taking the stairs and going through the main doors?" Freddie turns away from us to blow his smoke in the other direction, but at this point his entire arm is on my arm.

I push him off of me.

"No, I don't think so. The only front access is the main doors..." Her voice trails off. I stand up straighter. "There's another access. It's an emergency exit. Comes from the basement. We never use it."

I want to throttle her, but I resist the urge. Freddie snubs out his cigarette on the bar cart.

"You can get to the basement from here—" she goes to open the middle door. The one that leads to the hallway office when the door bursts open.

***

Freddie

Pretty little Ondine busts through the door, Sabbies was just about to walk through. She is so sweaty and frantic. Her cute little black dress is hanging off of her. She makes this high-pitched squeak and then hops into Sabbies's arms. God, she's so electric. She makes me hum whenever I'm near her.

Like a storm is about to hit.

"Man-ho," she sobs, "Man-ho is down there. Fifteen feral alphas."

Oh, isn't she just the *absolute* most helpful creature? I take a quick inventory. Unlike my brother, who was able to conjure a machete out of thin air, all I have are my mitts. But it's more than enough.

I waste not a second. I go right through the door she came from and run at top speed to the end of the hall and down some stairs. The further down I go, the less the de-scenters are working. I know what Man-ho smells like. Like death in a humid room. I follow that smell until I make it to an empty classroom. It reeks of alpha and Ondine's fear. I leave the room and find the door to the outside. It opens right up to the valet, where maybe 30 people wait for their cars.

Where the hell is Man-ho?

I'm going to fucking kill him.

Everything he does and is and stands for makes me want to remove his beating heart from his chest while he watches. I've been closing my eyes and picturing destroying this man for most of my life.

I weave through the crowd, and while his smell is everywhere, I can already tell he's gone. His smell is a beacon, though, to every feral male alpha in this crowd trying to hide amongst them. He's left men behind, thinking they'd blend into the crowd.

I grab a redhead by the nape of his neck and throw him to the ground. The crowd parts and shouts as I pump my fists into the guy, keeping him on the ground. His buddy tries to help, but I'm amped up.

I let his buddy pull me off of him. His hands are eating into the flesh on my shoulders, tearing at my clothing. Once I'm close to him and on my feet, I pivot and slam my knuckles into his ribs. He doubled over and I knee him in the groin.

I'm stronger than them.

I'm faster than them.

My whole world is centered on being better trained than them.

I know how Man-ho trains his pupils. The promises he makes them. The suffering he uses to hone their abilities. And I know their goddamned weaknesses.

I just wish I wasn't wearing dress shoes and slacks.

Blood sprays on my face as I slam a third man into a pillar holding up the awning over the oxbow driveway. Fuck yes. That's the fucking shit.

Several of the foul smelling fuckers jump into a car that pulls up. There's a car behind them, so I pop one of my victims in the mouth to move him out of the way, and rush up to the car. The car of alphas peels away from the building, and I'm already reaching in to roughly take out the valet on the other car. I apologize to the terrified beta and take his place behind the wheel. I'm out of the street in no time.

I call Jake as I'm rushing through traffic after the alphas.

"Jake, where the fuck is Man-ho?"

His voice is tight, but he's all business. "Not at the school. Not at his house."

I shake my head, realizing he doesn't know what just happened. "Man-ho was at the Club the whole time. He had Ondine in the basement with fifteen alphas trying to get a scent-match. Ondine got away, and I chased after the men. Man-ho was gone, but I took down a few guys. I'm chasing after some boat of a car with four of them. But I need Man-ho!"

"You lost him! You lost your mark!" Oh no, Jake is about to read me to filth. "You are his enemy, I thought. You are the one with his smell.

You want to kill him, and yet right under your nose, he took my omega, who was standing ten feet away from you! This is your fucking job, Freddie. Maybe you should go back to the mountains and meditate on how to take care of your own business, since actually doing it is outside of your grasp!"

Humbled, I stay quiet.

I grind my teeth in frustration. But I stay quiet.

"You're no longer my client, Freddie." His words hit me like a spear through the gut. I can't do this without him. I can't do this without his pack. If he's out, does that mean he'll take Ondine with him? If he's off this job, does that mean he is done with me entirely? He grumbles about twelve very not nice things about me and everyone else associated with me. "Get back to HQ. Now!"

I say I will and hang up the call.

"Fuck!" I scream into the windshield and hit the steering wheel over and over and over until my fists and chest hurt.

I rip my hand through my hair. He wants to meet at the room. He isn't completely done with me. I'll make this right. I'll set things straight. I can't let him turn me away, not now. Not now.

22

Dying. Dying. Dying.

Ondine

S abbies holds me close to him and breathes me in. I'm so relieved he's here. His phone rings, and he lets me go to answer it. I take my arms off of him and wrap them around myself. I'm pretty good at self-soothing. I tap my hands on my elbows, back and forth, and breathe deeply. The omega in me needs an alpha, especially now. A safe alpha. But I'm not even sure that's a real thing. A mass forms in my throat, and I can't swallow it down.

I shiver. I can't tell if it's cold in here, but my teeth are chattering.

Oh, it's probably adrenaline.

I remember when Sebastian told me that after Jake had attacked Shadow.

Where is Jake?

"Where's Jake?"

Sabbies is on his phone, talking to people and pacing around me.

My stomach cramps.

No. No. No.

Sweat drips down my forehead into my hairline.

No.

I know exactly what's happening. It's been happening my whole goddamned life. If I had anyone at all watching out for me, they would have told me what was going on much sooner. I used to just think it was the flu.

Here's a fun fact: there's actually no such thing as a beta transforming into an omega. She was an omega the whole time, just repressed. It can happen for a hundred different reasons. Whatever my reasons were, who knows, but I've been an omega my whole life, which means I know exactly what it feels like to have bond sickness.

I didn't know what it was until college, when the campus clinic was confused why a beta was showing signs of bond sickness. They were the first to propose the idea that I might actually be an omega. Until I perfumed—I didn't believe them.

All the blood rushes out of my feet and hands, leaving them empty and cold. Everything is tingling, and fear is rushing into the space left behind.

My stomach cramps again, and I whimper.

I can't go through this again.

"Where's Jake?" I whimper again, and Sabbies finally looks over to me.

"God, Ondine, you look white as a ghost," he says.

He meets my eyes, and something clicks.

He reaches for me, but I pull away. My insecurities rear their nasty head. He doesn't really want me.

My chest tightens like a heart attack.

It's one thing to go through bond sickness alone. Or surrounded by beta college students. It's another to have an alpha in front of you. I desperately try to breathe a full breath, but nothing goes through.

Bond sickness can kill an omega.

Am I going to die?

I think of the series of events that lead me here. Shadow denying me. Sabbies ignoring me for weeks. Jake offering me only him and not his pack. Having all those alphas smell me. All the words Man-ho said. As much as they didn't hurt me, they still hurt me. Having to push back on the alpha influence.

It's too much. I'm not designed to handle any of this.

An omega should be loved and cherished. They should be spoiled. They should be indulged. Touched. Fucked. Treasured. I don't even have a nest. My throat cramps from trying to suck in a breath.

I can feel my heart beating erratically.

"Ondine!" Sabbies shouts and tries for me again. Tears track down my face.

A woman from the club staff comes up to the two of us. I can hear her, but it's like she's far away. "She's an omega? She looks like she's having bond sickness."

"No, that's..."

The woman looks at him like he's a goddamn idiot. "Is she yours?"

He hesitates, and I cry out as my stomach cramps again. "She's...in placement with my pack."

She shakes her head. "Well, not to be an ass, but then you did this. She needs a nest. She needs your knot. She needs everything an omega needs. And now. Do you even know how to take care of an omega? Maybe you should take her to a clinic. They have emergency services."

And that's it for me. I sink to the ground.

I'm going to start convulsing soon.

I can't tell you the amount of times I woke up in my own vomit. I can't believe bond sickness hasn't killed me yet.

I drop my hands to the floor. It's best to try to relax, otherwise, I can hurt myself even more trying to stop it from happening.

And then something nice happens. Nothing ever nice happens. Sabbies drapes his jacket over my shoulders.

"You've got to get her out of here. The de-scenters prevent her from being comforted by your smell. Wait, does she even like your smell? I really think you should take her to a clinic."

Sabbies growls at the woman. "She likes my smell. I'm getting her out of here. Thank you for your help."

He picks me up in one motion and carries me down the stairs. I'm trying so hard to abate the convulsions. Once those happen, I will have no more control. I'm openly weeping. God, everything hurts. Nothing is going to be better. If I can't weather this, then I'll die. I'm dying. I'm dying dying dying.

23

Life Flight

Sebastian

I have sisters who are omegas, alpha brothers, and come from a large A/B/O clan, yet I've never seen bond sickness.

But then again, my sisters have always been spoiled and well taken care of. They have found alphas, and all left our home. It's not common to keep seeing your family after bonding, so I haven't seen some of them in years. Oh my god, if I ever found out one of them got bond sickness, I'd take Jake and Shadow, and we'd go murder every last one of them.

And here I am, with my own sick omega.

Ok, enough with the pity party.

Ondine and I are on the street. There are several grown men with blood on their faces and holding their bodies, wounded. Looks like Freddie made his way down here.

There's no way I'm getting a car in this melee.

There's an Omega Clinic nearby. Just a few blocks away. In the opposite direction is Sky Nest. They have suites with nests in them. I have to decide. If I took her to Sky Nest, she'd rely on me to get her through this.

Do I trust myself enough to help her?

I pull her face up and peel her eyelids back gently with my thumb. Her eyes are watery and pinkish all over. I let her close her eyes, and I cup her face, then lean in to kiss her forehead.

Earlier today, with Boone, he had practically convinced me that my fears are true—I'm not enough for her. He tried to convince me by bringing up Bunny. I don't know the details of that story, but it's not this story.

She's leaning on me, panting terribly. Her skin is thin and cold. Her body is shaking. She needs me.

There's this primal pull inside of me that says I have everything I need to care for her. Does she even know how much I want to show her what I can do for her?

I can help her. She's going to be ok.

Ondine whimpers, but it's involuntary and comes deep within her. It's a call to any alpha nearby to help her.

"Ondine, my heart, I've got you. Do you understand? You're going to be ok."

She doesn't react to me with positivity. She probably doesn't have any trust in me at all at this point. And I don't blame her.

I get her away from the Fine Bastian Club, away from the de-scenters. I smelled Freddie on the street, so it should be far enough, but I keep moving her further away, just in case.

I stop her and turn her shoulder so we are facing each other.

"Ondine, I'm going to scent you. Stop me if it's not what you want," I warn her in case she doesn't want me to. She gives me a little nod. I pull her closer and dip my head down. The alpha in me starts to come to life. I place my cheek on her cheek. I slide my face over hers until our necks are connecting. Then instinct fully takes over, and I run my skin over her. The contact relaxes me as it does her. I carefully draw her in so I can feel her reactions more closely. Her shoulders noticeably fall. Glorious. I lean into it more. I rub up her head and into her hair. My scent blooms around us and takes her over. She chases my touch with her body. That's a good sign. I move to her other side. One side isn't enough. She's sick. She needs as much as she can get. I know we are standing in the middle of the sidewalk on this random street, but this is an emergency. Scenting is a wholly private event. It's considered sexual. Doing it in public is crass.

But who fucking cares?

Her shaking has considerably lessened.

I'm breathing in and out, deep and long, pushing our chests together, getting her to mimic me. And she does.

"Good omega," I praise.

I wrap my arm around her shoulder and direct her to keep walking. We gotta get out of here.

My skin is buzzing. The air around us feels like a comfortable blanket. I think I needed the scenting as much as her.

We get to Sky Nest, and I take her to the lobby. I ask for a room with a nest. There's a small one in a different tower than where everyone is. I take it. I use the pack's credit card for the room.

The staff rushes away to get us nesting supplies. Every person who takes a look at this pale, sick omega knows exactly what's happening to her. I see some of the staff whisper to each other, asking if they should call the authorities.

A sick omega is a smoke signal to a larger problem. To get this bad means she's been mistreated for years. It's not something an omega gets because she's a bit needy or has been ignored a few times. It means Ondine has been suffering. She's been denied.

Omegas are the canary in the coal mine for how society is doing. The happier and well off their omega population, the better everyone is doing.

And not just that. They are rare. So, having a young, unbonded omega who's sick? Everyone has failed her.

Bond sickness is a result of being touch-starved, alpha-starved, hormone imbalanced, along with deep psychological stress.

But I'm going to take care of her.

We are going to get through this.

A group of staff members ushers us out of the elevator to the hall with nest rooms. They said it's pretty empty, and they've set us up without any neighbors. We make it around several bends and into our room. Staff unbox and remove packaging on all sorts of nesting materials. Blankets, pillows, and other soft things. They put slipcovers and pillowcases on new pillows they pull out of plastic. They ask me questions, and I direct them on what needs to happen.

One woman adjusts the lighting. A man puts new sheets on the bed, spraying it down with de-scenting spray.

They all look stressed and worried about Ondine.

I continue to rub and touch her wherever I can. She's too needy for me to hold back, and I don't. I'm running on instinct and everything I've been raised to be.

The room has a receiving room with couches and a tv with a table and chairs. There are two exits in the nest, one to a bathroom and one to the hallways. There's a double-king bed, low to the ground, and the staff are piling the nesting materials around.

"There's a fridge with snacks and drinks. Should we put in an order in the kitchen, Alpha Meier?" A woman asks me.

I wouldn't want to wait if she needs some food. "Yeah, some cold cuts would be great."

She nods, but pauses and says, "If she doesn't improve, don't hesitate to pick up the phone. The lobby can call emergency services. What's important is getting her better, ok?"

I growl. "I understand."

As soon as the door shuts on the last staff member, Ondine doubles over and vomits. I yank her to the bathroom and put her over the toilet. Her hair is short, so I have to hold it back with my whole hand. She vomits twice more before falling limp. She curls around the toilet.

"Fuck me," I huff. I grab some towels and clean up the vomit by the door. When that's done, I pull her up and clean her face, then make her swish some mouthwash.

She's so cold.

She's not talking. But I guess neither am I.

I lead her (carry her) to the nest and lay her down. My phone has buzzed a dozen times, so I finally pull it out.

So many texts and missed calls.

I call Jake.

"Sabbies, where the fuck are you? And why are your emotions so damned intense?! What is going on?" Hearing his voice relaxes me, even though he's yelling at me.

"Jake, what's going on with everyone?"

I adjust her body over the pillows and continue to pet her. Over her breasts. Up her neck. Down her thighs.

He sighs. "I'm firing Freddie as a client. This is a shit show. I'm almost at Sky Nest. I want everyone there. Shadow is here with me. I threw his machete into the river, but he wasn't upset at all, so I think he's got a second one. Freddie said you have Ondine?"

She's lying on her side while I cage her in. She's chasing my touches.

"It's bad," I say, at a loss for words.

"How bad did Man-ho hurt her?"

"Man-ho? I think this is more than that. Jake, she has bond sickness. I got her in a room at Sky Nest."

There's silence.

"Ondine has bond sickness?"

I can hear Shadow in the background asking him if he heard what he thinks he heard. Ondine looks like death is at her door. I nuzzle my nose into the space below her ear.

"No, no, no! Fuck! Where are you going?" Jake shouts at Shadow. "Fuck, Shadow just jumped out of the car at a red light. I'm hanging up. I'll be there soon. Take care of her Sabbies or I swear to god."

Of course, I'll take care of her. Ondine needs me. Her little tongue comes out and licks my wrist.

Jake ends the call. I toss the phone off the bed.

An alpha purr emits from my chest and sings to her. She looks so small. So vulnerable. I pull away, and she whines.

"It's ok, my heart. We need less clothing. I'm just taking off my clothes." I stand up to unbuckle my belt and slide off my shoes. I take everything off and lay it on a puff thing nearby. Then I take her dress off. She has these sexy little black panties on. It's a thong. Her bra comes off last. We are both naked. I lift her up and pull her to the center of the bed.

I settle in on her side and curl around her. She fits into my lap, lying on her side perfectly. I lay my arm across her. Her skin is ice. But it feels good, actually. I use my hand to touch her in a few places, seeing if she's tense.

My hand rests on her hip.

"You did so well tonight, escaping Man-ho all on your own. But I saw this," I say and hold up her right hand. Her thumb is all bruised up. "You don't know how to punch, do you? I'm impressed you tried, anyway. When you are feeling better, I'll teach you." I put her hand back down. Careful not to jostle it. Omegas heal very fast—she probably won't even have bruises later. "Tell me how you're feeling, Ondine."

She gulps, and her lips part. "How do you think I'm feeling?"

"Oh, sarcasm, that's real nice, Ondine."

I chuckle and then pull her tight into me, pushing my partial erection (I know) onto her ass. She burrows down, rubbing her head under my chin, and her ass against my cock.

"Better," she amends her first answer. I smile and breathe her in. Her vanilla scent is faint. "Why are you doing this? Does it make you hate me?"

Her words cause me to short-circuit.

"I don't hate you." I suck in a breath and add, "I could never hate you."

I have this desire to lick her. And if I know anything about alpha/omega pairings, it's that you can run entirely on instinct, and it usually works out. So, I do. I push her forward so I can lick her spine and shoulders. It makes my purring louder, and she's responding with all sorts of great noises.

I must hit a really good spot because she sucks in a breath and her legs dance.

I do it again, just to see if I imagined it, but sure thing her legs dance, but this time she throws her head back.

"Please, Sabbies," she breathes.

"You want me to touch you?"

"Touch my pussy," she clarifies. The bold part of me takes over, and I glide my hand over her ass to her front and then push my middle finger into her pussy. I need to see how wet she is. She's panting as I feel nothing but smooth, wet slick. I lick her back again, and she clamps her thighs together, trapping my hand.

I growl. "Open your legs, Omega."

I get both my arms under her and pull her on top of me. She's facing the low ceiling, and my knees help open her up.

"Please," she says. "Please."

"Please, what, little omega?"

"Make me feel good, Sabbies."

That I can do. I wrap my arms around her body to hold her still, and my hard cock is well between her legs and nowhere near her pussy. Instead, I use my finger to spread her lips apart and then sink my finger into her warmth. Her face is right near mine, so every reaction she has, I can feel, taste, hear, and smell. Her hands are on my forearm, holding on for dear life. I kiss her ear and then whisper, "Use these hands to stop me if you need a break."

She nods between her panting and whimpering.

I dive two fingers into her pussy all the way in and hook them so I stroke her inner walls. She screams out in pleasure, and I drown in the sound. Her feet push down on my knees, and I hold my legs stiff so she can use them however she needs.

With her mouth hanging open like that, I can't help myself. With my other hand, I hold her jaw and then press my thumb down onto her tongue. She groans in pleasure. I add a third finger to her pussy, and I don't take it slow.

My girl needs this.

Three fingers pump inside her, and the heel of my hand grinds down onto her clit.

She comes, and it's the most beautiful thing to hold a woman, so in her pleasure, as she comes for you. But I don't slow down. I continue to fuck her with my fingers and hold her as tightly as possible. Tears run down her cheeks, and I lick them up as fast as they fall. I wring another climax out of her. I want a third. I want more, and she wants just as much. Her fingernails dig into my forearm, but I don't stop. I let her mouth go so I can pinch and pull her nipples. She doesn't hold back on telling me how much she wants this, too.

I continue to pump, pinch, and lick—earning me a third orgasm from my beautiful omega.

Why haven't we been doing this the whole time? I was a fool to leave her to Shadow and Jake. She's mine. She's been mine the whole time. Fuck me. I ease my fingers out to give her a break, but it won't be for long. I want to show her exactly what it means to be mine.

I put her on her side, but she's still on top of me, so she can curl into a little ball. I don't ever stop touching her.

She whispers, like she's admitting a secret, "Jake asked me to be his. Not yours or Shadow's. Just his. Is that because you didn't want me?"

Her body temperature drops slightly. I rub her arm more fervently. "He didn't say anything to us, Ondine. He didn't ask. But if he did, I'd tell him you're already mine."

And it rings true. I only say what I know to be true. She's mine. I scrape my sharp alpha teeth over her skin. Her scent finally perfumes a little bit, so it's not just vanilla, but that cool, creamy note that makes my mouth water. I do it again, pressing my sharp teeth into her skin, just enough to feel how sharp they are, and I have to hold her still. "I need you to listen. I know Jake likes to fuck you in his office, and I love being part of that. But let me tell you what I want. I want to hold your hand. I want to laugh with you. I want to court you." I kiss her shoulders and neck. "You are too good for me or my pack. I'll do my best to make it worth it to be with me, Ondine. I'll make it worth it."

Our skin feels like one flesh. Our breaths are totally in sync now. She's mine. And she's going to be ok.

There's a knock at the door. I can't let her go. I can't leave her. But I have to.

I decide right there that I'm always going to take care of her. She'll never get this way again.

I detach myself from her reluctantly and throw some blankets over top of her. She burrows into them. I race to the front door and yank it open quickly. Jake and Freddie come barreling in. They are holding blankets and sheets in their arms, probably brought from the suite.

Freddie looks right at my dick. Then raises his eyebrows.

"Where is she?" Jake asks.

"The nest." I lead them to her. Jake undresses immediately. We enter the dark, low-ceiling room of the nest. Three alphas and one very sick omega. Freddie has blood on his face. He's just like Shadow. These fucking brothers. I stand with my hands on my hips. Observing as Jake gets completely nude and pulls the blankets off Ondine.

He growls, and his chest starts to emit a loud purring noise. "Ondine, baby, I'm here. I'm here. What happened?"

He pulls her out of her fetal position and makes her face him. "Jake, I don't feel well."

"I know, baby. Did Sabbies help?"

"He cleaned up my throw up," she tells him with her sweet voice, and my body shudders. "He kissed me."

We did more than that, and I can tell she wants to say it out loud, but she just can't get it out.

Jake turns to me and says, "She needs us to lie with her, skin-to-skin, and purr if we can. And we need to tell her how much we need her." I know this. All of her filters are down. We have to be open with her. If she were in a clinic, they'd sedate her and do scent therapy. It's not as effective as a pack of alphas doing exposure therapy. "And absolutely no biting. If we were to bond her right now, it would be unstable."

He doesn't need to tell me.

"Freddie, you aren't invited. Get out there and make sure everything is ok. Take our phones."

"Got it," he agrees quickly. I look at him to search for any hint that he's not fully invested. He seems like he's taking this seriously.

I turn back to Ondine and Jake. They pull me without me even asking. There's this hazy cloud of lust all around us, and my hindbrain takes over. The three of us are familiar with each other. And both Jake and I know to focus on the omega. So it's easy. It's easy to pull her between us and get her riled up further and further. My fingers on her nipples, his on her clit. His mouth is on her neck, and she and I are making out. Jake directs me to where I need to be to enter her.

"More," she moans over my lips. "More, please. I need more."

Jake asks, "You want us both in your pussy, greedy omega?"

She nods her head and then wraps her arms around my neck. Jake pushes us together and back. I widen my legs so he can get closer. He's going to fuck her with me inside. I hold her close and tighten my grip so she stays still.

Jake continues to push Ondine into me as he aligns our dicks together. I pick Ondine up and glide her up and down my cock. It only takes a few tries before she's wrapped around my entire cock and the tip of Jake's.

She rests her head on my shoulder and sucks on my neck. This is amazing. This is perfect. She's moaning into my skin how much she agrees that the sensation is out of control good.

I hold her still again, and Jake starts pumping in and out slowly, getting further and further into her every time.

"So tight," he says to us.

So fucking tight. Fucking fuck fuck. I hold all my muscles still so I don't accidentally come too soon. We gotta get her to come like this. With both our cocks inside her. But all I can do is hold her tight. She's panting into my neck, and her body is shaking. She's also saying, "Yes, yes, yes."

Jake is fully seated inside her. We both are. Minus our knots. I have never felt a sensation like this. It feels like a joining. I can feel both of our pulses against me.

"Ondine," Jake stutters, barely holding it together. "You come first, Ondine. Then Sabbies and I. Then we will push our knots into you."

I feel Jake's hand between us as he gets to her clit. I adjust to give him room, but the sensation is too much. Jake is still pumping in and out as he pinches Ondine's clit. He rubs it quickly in tight little circles. How on earth am I going to hold it together? I breathe in deep, but all I smell is that birthday cake, vanilla ice cream smell along with my own orange scent. We smell fucking amazing together.

Ondine bucks between us as Jake brings her to climax. That's it, that's what I need to let go. I'm coming, too. Jake is still fucking us, but now it's messy and wet and incredible.

My heart pinches, and my leg cramps as nirvana is reached. I shout as I come.

Ondine pulls her head back and also screams her pleasure. I watch as she tilts her head back down to make direct eye contact. God, she's so beautiful. The prettiest I've ever seen. "You're so incredible. You take us so well. Oh my god, Ondine, you were made for us."

Her eyes dart to the side and stay there. A shy smile builds on her face. I turn to see what she's looking at, and I nearly swallow my tongue.

Freddie never left the room.

As my sex addled brain tries to figure out what I'm looking at, Jake comes. He holds onto Ondine and I tightly. Bruising us both, no doubt. Ondine is still smiling.

Freddie looks feral. I should have made sure he left, but everything happened too fast. I pull out of Ondine as Jake pushes his growing knot into her. My knot is also growing, but I won't knot her. I have to get Freddie out of here. He can go into a feral rage. I kiss the omega as I pull away from her.

Ondine is unbonded. So is Freddie. His hand is on the door handle, like he intends to leave. His other hand holds our phones. I'm trying desperately to catch my breath. Freddie's eyes lock on mine. He drops the phones, lets go of the door, preparing to attack. I push out of the nest and leap towards him, meeting him halfway.

24

Crimson Lion

Shadow

J ake tosses my machete out the window and (presumably) into the river. But little does he know I have a second one on me. When I saw Man-ho's fleet vehicles in the front of the Fine Bastian Club, I put it all together very quickly. I didn't go through four years of military college, then two years of special forces training to be a fucking idiot. He'd come for Ondine.

Jake had lost his mind the day Ondine went to the city to get her haircut, and it didn't take long for me to realize he'd *feared* for her. The omegas that had been taken were all taken near Chinatown, which is in the center of the city, which narrows it down to one horrible man—Alpha Lee Man-ho. Cynthia, who works intimately with Man-ho, saw Ondine in our hotel room. Unbonded, young, beautiful—but she didn't take into account her affiliations.

And maybe they didn't take that into account because the Meier Protection Group is not openly courting her. We are temporarily contracted. We set ourselves up for this to happen.

A temporary placement is either a trial or a hormone balance therapy. We are more so the latter. We have very little claim on her.

Legally speaking.

But I don't really care what's legal when the alpha in me is snapping his jaws and throwing his body against the confines of its mortal flesh to seek absolution.

Man-ho took my omega for a scent test. He wanted to take her from me. From my alphas. He dies.

Tonight.

Jake and I were at the school and at his residence. That leaves the Crimson Lion the best bet on where the dead-man-walking ran off to.

As soon as I hear that Ondine slipped into bond-sickness after the scent test, that does it for me. I open the car door and roll out. Jake yells after me. But it's not like I haven't done this before. He keeps driving, like a good alpha, to his omega. Ondine doesn't need me in her nest. She needs me to enact her revenge. I'm scraped up a little, but I leap to my feet and get off the riverfront bypass. I wish I could contact Sabbies. He's great with directions. He'd be able to easily tell me how to get to the Crimson Lion from here. I have to take a second to orient myself by running down some streets. I finally get my coordinates right and then keep running to Chinatown.

The Crimson Lion is not just a restaurant. It's a market square with several restaurants above and below the square. Anything, from a quick lunch at windows to fine dining. When Freddie met with him the other day, it was in the fine dining room. But I bet anything he'll be at his more regular haunt in the back of the 24/7 cafe.

I slow my pace so I can start regulating my heart rate and get a smart hold on my breath. I don't want to be red in the face or neck when I meet a powerful alpha. I need to appear cool.

I pump my fists to force the blood out of them.

I round the corner. The street signs change from English to hanzi, Chinese characters. The streetlights turn from cool to warm. The sounds and smells all shift to feel like home. I grew up nearby here.

My parents moved a few times, so it's not home now, but it still feels like my childhood. I'm single-minded, though, so I don't let it distract me. I enter the Crimson Lion market square. The night market is open and crowded tonight. I mark all my exits. I locate where all of Man-ho's security is posted. They are here to keep certain folks out and thefts to a minimum. Or to settle disputes. Not one of them notices me.

The cafe is nearly empty. When I enter, two betas posted at the door and try to give me a mean-mug to indicate I need to leave. If I were there for tea or soup, it would work. But I'm here for their boss. I stand between them right in front of the entrance, in a strong position. My black duster is open, showing off my suit and tie. My hair is tied tightly at the back of my neck. My hands are empty.

"Alpha Lee Man-ho," I call out in a big, powerful voice. I lace the sound with my alpha bark. It's enough to showcase I have power, though it doesn't really *do* anything. There's a curtain at the back of the cafe that I know leads to another room. One where he is most likely settled. "It is Shadow Meier, half-brother to Freddie Wong, and alpha to Omega Ondine. I've come to talk to you."

Two older alphas emerge from the back. I resist the urge to smile triumphantly as they nod their head to the back, indicating I can enter.

I make sure to look each one in the eye. I want them to know I know their faces. They stop me before going through the curtain so they can pat me down. They find a holstered gun at my ankle and my ribs. I pull them out and hand them over. My Glock and my J-frame. It's fine. They didn't find my machete.

My J-frame isn't even loaded.

They finish their inspection and hold the curtain open for me. I tell them thank you and enter the moody, low-ceilinged room. It's still not the room I need. Nothing illegal happens here. Just thugs who want privacy. I continue to the back and walk down a set of stairs. At the bottom, a smiling young woman greets me. She opens the door to the realm of the underworld. Gambling tables. Unregulated drug sales and use. Prostitution. Strippers.

But I zero in on Lee Man-ho at the back, sitting in a round booth.

I can smell at least two omegas in the room. Plenty of alphas. And the rest betas. Mostly men. They want the people in here contained. There's only one way in and one way out. But Man-ho wouldn't be in a room like that. I'd guess the curtain behind his booth is holding an exit. I'd also guess the part of the room where two beta bodyguards are hovering is near another exit. I note the camera since the guards dart their eyes to it without thinking.

"Alpha Wong," Man-ho calls out to me as I stalk to his table. The rest of the tables and the platforms of dancing girls go quiet. The DJ lowers the music.

"It's Meier."

"My apologies, Alpha Meier. Didn't realize you let yourself get leashed. Is it a degradation kink? Alphas that kneel to lesser alphas have always fascinated me. I think it comes down to sexual depravity. Wouldn't you say?"

God, I forgot how chatty this mother fucker is. As quick as a lightning strike, I pull a tactical throwing knife and lodge it into the table in front of Man-ho. The other patrons with him jump up and run out of the booth, but he stays put. Unaffected.

"You took my omega and subjected her to a scent test."

"I did," he says proudly. "And I'll do it again, Alpha Meier. I will find her a match among my men. You cannot stop me with your little knives or your scary bark."

Silence sits between us. I kick my eyebrow up, happy he's given me a chance to talk. I thought for sure he'd launch into another speech.

"No, you will not. Not only will I demand your punishment right here and right now. But you will never come near my omega ever again."

He looks so cool as he clicks his tongue and asks, "You won't demand I stop trying to sever the head from the shoulders of your mother's alpha, Senator Wong?"

I guess he's right to point out I came here for Ondine, and not Senator Wong.

Again, he lets silence sit between us.

He's stalling me.

He is afraid of me! The thought is going to make my ego huge. Enough talking then. I throw two more knives at him. Both entering his shoulders. He falls back into the false door behind him, but I'm already leaping across the table to fall into the door with him.

We crash down a fucking chute that leads into an adjacent hallway. I've got my knees tucked up, so when we crash into the hallway, I just need to pop them out to kick him with both feet in the stomach.

He gurgles and grunts as I get my footing back and roll away.

When I stand, I have my machete in my fist. He's not standing up, though. He's crumpled up on the ground. Oh my god. He's knocked out. Before I can second guess myself, I put away my machete and haul the man up. His limp giant body is near impossible to move, but I'm running on pure adrenaline.

I get him into an empty office and shut the door. Keeping the light off. I pull him onto a chair and tie his legs and arms to it with cabling from a box near the door.

Then I spit on him.

I call Jake.

I need him to decide if we take a finger, a hand, or I just end this now and kill him.

25

Primal Fear

Freddie

I've felt fear many times in my life. I've stood on the edge of absolute dread and danger time and time again. As a born feral alpha, it's always been wrapped up in my fate. Being feral is going to always be with me. I've accepted it. The amount of times in my life I've blacked out to find I've done great violence should be reason enough to never allow me near this vulnerable, sweet omega.

She's the scariest thing I've ever come across.

And I should never have had her alone in the woods that night.

I lied to Jake. He knew it too, that's why he stopped listening to me while I told him my story.

I found my scent match that night.

And I took her.

She doesn't remember, though, because the poor girl perfumed that night for the first time.

The fear I felt escaped me like a mushroom cloud. She'd wandered on the edges of the party, and I grabbed her. She barely resisted. She seemed curious. She was beautifully submissive. Her mouth under my hand didn't even protest. I wanted to melt away with her.

And it was me who was afraid and not the princess I stole.

I took her away, pushed her up against a boulder, and kissed her. She lit me aflame. Her hands went under my shirt. My hands were in her wig.

And then, triggered by the sound of my alpha purr, she perfumed. She passed out in my arms. I didn't know what was happening at first. I held her and drank in her incredibly vibrant and bright scent. After a while, when the haze settled, I realized what had happened. I needed to get out of there. I was in no position to take an omega.

I brought her back to her party and laid her in the cab of her boyfriend's truck.

That was one year ago. I smelled her on Jake when I arrived in the city and knew she was back in my life.

I've spent all this time trying to be the kind of alpha who could care for her. But seeing how obsessed Jake is. How Shadow looks at her like she hung the moon. And how Sebastian talks about her like she's everything. I realized she's found a pack.

They are a good pack. And Jake is a strong alpha.

I've taken so many hormones to stop my scent from becoming a problem for her. It's a wonder I'm even standing.

I could tell the moment they wore off tonight, when Sebastian noticed my scent. And I couldn't get enough of him. I was this close to licking him tonight.

This room smells like vanilla, cake, and orange ice cream. Whiskey-tinged. Smokey and creamy. God, I am going to come in my pants just from the smells alone. I could bury myself in these scents until I die and die happy.

Ondine is looking at me with want. And my alpha side is howling at me to take her. To fuck her. Bite her. Claim her. I shouldn't be here.

I feel myself getting washed away in the primal desires of my feral alpha side, and I'm powerless to stop it. I want to fuck. I need to fuck. And I must fuck her.

Sabbies sees the alpha in me. And my alpha loves the attention. He wants him just as badly. Whatever I'm holding in my hands gets abandoned. But as I'm trying to get to my omega, I'm halted entirely. My back hits the floor with such a great force, it knocks the air out of me, and I can't breathe. I gasp for a breath I can't have.

Sabbies pulls me off the floor and into the hallway, slamming the door shut behind us. Cutting me off from Ondine. He hauls me to the receiving room with the windows and throws me on a couch.

He bares his teeth at me.

"*No!*" he barks. My alpha just shrugs off his influence. It's paltry compared to mine. I bare my teeth back, but with no threat. He's a fine consolation prize. He doesn't know this, so he holds my shirt tight in his fists and slams me up and down into the soft couch. His naked body holds me down. He smells like Ondine and sex and fucking and orange dreams. I'm so fucking hard.

He finally pauses. He feels how hard I am. Of course I am. I'm about to go into a feral rut. He smells the air and notices my intentions are not violent. Only sexual. I cock my eyebrow.

"You can't go in there with her. You can't be trusted to only fuck her and not bite her. And most importantly, Jake just knotted her," he says so logically. Oh, sweet Sebastian. Always does the right thing. Always expects everyone around him to obey the rules, made up or otherwise. "You need to keep it together."

I playfully snap at him, and he throws his head back, but stays, pinning me down with all his strength.

"And you don't want to help me? Did she fuck everything out of you?"

Mate of my mate, the alpha in me says. It startles me so much I lose my smile. Is Sebastian also her scent match? His scent does send me into a tailspin. It's so similar to how I feel around the omega. I realize Sabbies hasn't declined my offer.

I watch him gulp a dry mouth. I look into his eyes. He's not opposed. I'm so hard I'm aching.

His mouth hangs open a little, and I can't help but look at his lips. Is he into men? I close my eyes. Who fucking cares?

Suddenly, I feel his mouth on mine. It's unsure, but there's a ferocity to it. Sabbies is kissing me. With tongue. I get in the game and kiss him back. My alpha loves this unexpected kiss. I fucking love it too. It makes not having Ondine right now not the worst thing.

Sabbies is fiddling with my pants. I am so lost in the kiss, it takes me way too long to realize he's trying to get my pants off. Freddie, get it together.

I get my pants pulled down enough to pull my cock out. Sabbies is hard and right there, so I grab us both and give them a nice up and down motion. We both groan into our mouths.

He adjusts himself on top of me more, and now I've got a great grip on our cocks. While he continues to kiss me like it's the most important thing he's ever done, I stroke our cocks hard and fast, trying to elicit the most intense sounds. And I'm really good because both of us are very vocal.

I started down this path, but it's my inner alpha that takes it from here. He wants sex and fucking and rutting and pleasure. And he'll get it. He'll take it from Sebastian Meier.

Time bends and slows and stops and warps—but it's all hot breaths, tongue and teeth clashing, and our bodies writhing together.

I chase our shared climax all the way through it. We both shutter and kick and moan and shout. I cannot stop kissing him throughout it all.

In the descent, like we'd climbed a tall mountain, we just pant into each other's mouths. I hold our cocks together with cum coating my entire hand. I cannot believe I just did that with Sabbies. Is Shadow going to be pissed? My little brother's best friend...fucking hell, Freddie.

Does he regret it?

He looks like he can't even think straight. Well, that's probably a good thing.

We both hear him at the same time–Jake. He's on the phone. He steps out of the nest, using the door down the hall. Sabbies leaps off of me and is suddenly on the other side of the room. I get off the couch and stand there. I tuck my cock into my slacks and fasten them back on just as Jake walks in.

Fuck this.

I exit to the bathroom and lock the door behind me.

26

Please, Freddie

Jake

She's passed out in my arms. My knot is going down, but I want to stay inside her. She's everything to me. I never want to let her go. She's going to be mine. I'll bite her into my pack in her next heat. By then, she'll be healed and ready for me. A bonding bite done during a heat is the strongest one. I would never accept anything less for her.

My phone rings and I peek out to see it sitting on the floor. Why is my phone on the floor? Sebastian's phone is next to it.

Its obnoxious ring could wake the omega, and I need her to rest. I slip out of her, and a little frown forms on her face. I kiss the edge of her mouth, and her face softens again. I ease out of the nest and cover her with blankets.

I answer the phone as Shadow calls in.

"Where are you?" I ask first, whispering.

"Crimson Lion."

I shut my eyes and sigh.

He continues, "I have Man-ho tied to a chair. Should I kill him?"

This isn't the first, nor will it be the last time Shadow has been in this situation, and I've been on the other side of this call. So I go through my questions:

"Who knows, you're there?"

I hear the hiss in his voice. "A lot of people."

"They know it's you?"

"I announced myself."

"Best not to kill him then. Want to stab his knee?" I offer.

He makes a sad little noise.

"I'm sorry, buddy. But you can't announce yourself as the killer in a crime."

But I hear yelling, and he says, "Tell Sebastian I need an extraction. I'm a little trapped in here."

"How much time?"

"Give me 00:20."

The line goes dead.

Shit.

I'm thirsty. And hungry. I check on Ondine, and she looks asleep. I put on my pants and leave the nest.

Sebastian and Freddie are in the receiving room. Out of breath and on either side of the room. It smells like spent in here. Did they…fool around?

Sebastian doesn't meet my eyes. Freddie heads into the bathroom and shuts the door.

"Sabbies?" I ask as I find the fridge with water and snacks. But when I look around, I see a tray of sandwiches and things. "Come eat."

"I'm sorry," Sebastian says.

I meet his eyes. He *was* out here messing around with Freddie. "Come here and eat. You've had a long night."

If he fucked Freddie, I know he had good reason. I don't need to be nose deep up the asshole of every member of my pack. There's no reason for him to feel guilty.

I make him a sandwich with ham and turkey on a roll. He takes it graciously from me.

"Shadow needs an extraction. He went after Man-ho for what he did to Ondine. He's at the Crimson Lion. Here's your phone," I say as I hand him his phone. Sebastian gets right to work getting a team together for the extraction. I do the same thing and pull up my map and get to work on a plan with a roll hanging halfway out of my mouth.

***

Freddie

I stand in the dark bathroom listening to Jake and Sebastian talk through the door. Jake isn't mad, but he suspects what we were up to. I've got to say, of all the times I had a scare with my feral nature, so far this one has had the least damaging results. There's another door to the back of the bathroom that leads into the nest, and I hear it slowly opening.

My whole body stiffens.

Oh, fuck.

I stay perfectly still as I hear the little pads of Ondine's feet on the tile move toward me. She sidles up next to me and mocks, putting her ear to the door.

"What're we listening to?" she asks in a very quiet voice. She turns to look up at me.

She's here.

My heart.

"Just making sure I'm not going to be thrown out of here," I tell her.

Her head tilts to the side, confused. It's so damned cute. I shrug.

Her nostrils flare, having caught a scent. She looks down at my hand, the one covered in cum. She takes my wrist and pulls my hand up closer to her face, then closes her eyes and breathes in deeply.

Fuck me.

She smells mine and Sebastian's cum. And then, before I can wrap my head around this situation, she licks my hand from the palm up my thumb. I press my thumb into her tongue, and she lets out a small moan.

"Wow."

Ondine, holding my wrist, leads me to her nest, and I am at her mercy.

***

Ondine

I remove Freddie's shirt, and he shrugs off his slacks. I lay back into the pillows on the bed, and he lies next to me, never breaking eye contact.

Freddie pulls me into him, our legs interlacing. I bury my face in his neck.

He smells like magic, but it's buried under a pile of oranges.

"You smell like Sabbies," I say. He tasted like him, too. While Jake and I were in here, I guess they were out there. "Did you two..."

"He helped me. Seeing you with them—I was about to go into a feral rut. He helped me."

Sabbies helped me, too. He helped me not slide into complete oblivion. Breathing Freddie in is helping ease the pain of bond-sickness, but his smell keeps escaping me, like a rabbit in the briars.

He smells like someone is making tea, but somewhere far away. A strong English tea. In a teacup I want.

You know what would really ease the pain—Freddie's cock. I absentmindedly grind my hips into him.

"Freddie," I say, and I hope he knows it's a question, a demand, a plea.

"Princess, I cannot help you. Not with that."

I don't like that. But if he's saying no, he's saying no. I stop my movements and pull away to create some space.

"No, no, no," Freddie shifts, so he's over me, holding my face, but I won't make eye contact.

"We can just lie here, Freddie. Your body heat and scent are still helping." I'm trying really hard not to feel rejected.

"Princess, no. I want you so bad it hurts. I'm, fuck, I don't know how to say this—I'm feral, Ondine. Feral. Do you know what that means? You're an omega. If I fuck you, I'll go into a rut. I'll black out, and I won't be able to stop myself from taking all my satisfaction—using you. I'll become possessive and violent. And who knows when I'll be able to come out of it."

Honestly, that sounds exactly like what I need. I imagine the little bits of possession Sabbies shows or Jake. How the omega in me salivates. I think she'd do just fine with a feral alpha.

I'm humping him again.

"Ondine, listen, you're unbonded and so am I. There'd be no one to stop me from giving you a claim. From biting you. I'd knot you and bite you and claim you—"

He's warning me, but I moan so loud you'd think I came. He's turning me on so badly that I ache in every single sexual part of my body, which at this point is every part of my body.

"Yes. Knot me, bite me, claim me, Freddie."

Freddie bares his teeth at me and growls, making me speed up. I'm going to come dry humping this man.

"You don't know what you're saying."

He kisses my face and jaw with little pecks.

I open my eyes and lock them with his oil slick gaze. Drool pools on the side of Freddie's mouth. I rear up and lick his lips.

"I can't fuck you," he says again, and my face crumbles, and I can't stop the tears. Then why is he nearly naked and on top of me?! I push him away with all my pathetic might. "Stop! Let me finish! I can't fuck you without telling you everything. Ok, so *listen*!"

He used his alpha bark, so even if I wanted to kick him off of me, I couldn't.

"I know you. We've met. I didn't know that you hadn't perfumed until that night. And I didn't know what came over me, Ondine. I didn't know."

My whole body goes still.

That night.

What is he saying?

The night I perfumed?

Graduation night.

Oh my god.

I would have told this story much differently if I didn't know about Freddie. I would have talked about how I lost my mind and hallucinated an alpha stealing me away from my friends and causing my heart to seize. My skin to catch fire. My core to clamp. It felt like I was morphing into a goddamned werewolf. And yet it was the most pleasure I'd ever felt in my life. I was surrounded by love. All my dreams were coming true in one moment. I'd found someone to be with me forever. Love and care for me. And then I woke up in the back of my boyfriend's truck alone.

Freddie Wong was there the night I turned into an omega?

My back suddenly bows, and I cry out in pain.

I need. I need more. Everything in me and outside of me needs. I feel disconnected. Rejected. Alone. I need.

"Please," I whimper. "Please."

"Fuck me, Ondine. This is such a bad idea. Jake is going to kill me. You're going to kill me. I won't be able to stop myself. I don't want to hurt you. I'm going to ruin everything. I'm not worthy of you. I'm not supposed to be here with you. You deserve so much more than me." He's talking, but thankfully, he's taking off his briefs and stroking his hands over my hot and cold skin and breasts. He pinches my nipples. Thank you for everything. His fingers pass over my pussy, and they come back shiny. He's making these delicious sex noises while also telling me how bad of an idea this is.

My legs are on either side of him, I'm lying back, and he's kneeling before me. He grabs his dick and rubs the tip against my pussy.

"Yes! Yes! Fuck yes. Please, Freddie. Please."

"God, this pussy smells like Sebastian, Jake, and you. This is going to kill me alone," Freddie mutters.

He hisses and grunts and then falls forward, his hand on the mattress next to my head. I push up on him, grinding my hips. Please god, just let me have one fucking thing. One thing. I never ask for anything. Let me have this.

His necklace dangles in front of me, and I reach up and finger the chain. His eyes dart to mine, and I smile while slowly pulling.

The closer I get the necklace to me, the more pressure he puts on my entrance.

And then he's lost, and so I am.

I remember pressure and pain and the utmost pleasure.

I remember only satiation as my mate bonds me with his bite.

27

Mate

Jake

Sabbies sits naked on the couch and reviews the radio channels as his team communicates. The program transcribes it so he can visually see all the chatter at once. Shadow has a highly intelligent tracker, so we can track him using x, y, and z coordinates, so it shouldn't be long until they get to him. I open another water bottle and drink half of it.

"This is a fucking disaster," I say out loud. Not about Shadow and his mission. But about Ondine falling into bond-sickness. "We've failed that girl over and over. What made us think we could do this?" I'm usually never this vulnerable and pitiful. But he is my pack, and if I can't be honest with him, then I'm a shit pack lead. "Ok, enough of that." I wipe my hands together in a few claps.

I collect a plate with a bread roll, cheese, and rolled up ham, and grab a plastic water bottle.

"Maybe she will eat or drink something. We should get back in there."

He nods his head.

"Jake, everything is going to be ok. She's already improving. She knows we want her. When we get back to our place, we need to tell her we want to court her. Properly."

I nod. I know he's right. Everything will be ok.

He stands and walks over to me. I open my arms and he hugs me while I hold the plate and water. He pulls away while slapping my back.

We head down the hall and open the door to the nest.

And reveal a fucking nightmare.

Ondine is being dominated by Freddie fucking Wong, whose jaws are open and moments away from biting her neck. What the fuck am I looking at? All the blood runs out of my hands, preparing for a fight. I'm angry. Furious. I'm going to kill him. Before my next breath, the food has been abandoned, and I have my hand on Freddie's face, pulling him back, and my arm around his waist, yanking him off of her.

I don't even think about whether he has knotted her. But it's obvious he hasn't when I've got him pinned to the wall. Ondine screams belatedly.

"Did he bite her?!" I shout at Sebastian. He pulls open Freddie's jaw and face, tipping his mouth towards him, investigating his teeth.

Ondine is screaming. Her short, panicked sobs aren't stopping.

Sebastian gasps. "There's blood! There's blood on his teeth!"

My heart drops out of my chest.

I release Freddie and shove him in Sebastian's arms and go to Ondine. My knees slide against the bed, and I pull her towards me. My hands search her pretty skin. There better not be a mark. THERE BETTER NOT FUCKING BE A MARK!

On her skin, right where her shoulder meets her neck, there's a mark. It's shallow. It's slight. I'd pulled him off before he could sink them in too far. But she's bleeding.

He's bitten her. He's bonded her. He's TAKEN HER AWAY FROM ME!

And then a second thought, he's bitten an omega in bond-sickness.

"You cannot bond an omega with bond-sickness!" I turn my head and yell at Freddie. "It's unstable. It's fractured. You could kill her!" It could also kill Freddie, but that would be the best outcome here.

Watching Freddie, I don't see any signs he's listening. I see things much, much worse. He's in rut. He's snapping his jaws at my Sebastian. His veins are popping out and visible across his body.

He just bonded with Ondine.

He's feral.

And we are in his mate's nest.

Ondine weeps below me. I stroke her face, pushing her hair out of it. I pull her up and lick her tears off her cheeks, whispering my promises that I will make this right. She moves closer to my chest, and I realize I'm purring for her.

I run my thumb over the apple of her cheek.

I'm a bad alpha. How did I let this happen?

Sebastian has wrestled Freddie to the ground and put him in a half-nelson.

I pull Ondine closer. She's compliant. She molds into my body, seeking warmth. I sigh and wrap my arms around her, holding her in my whole body.

Sebastian asks, "Ondine, how do you feel?"

"I just want my alpha," she mumbles into my chest. My heart breaks when I realize she doesn't mean me. She grips my biceps so hard and cries, "I need Freddie. Why did he leave me?"

As much as I want her to need me, I'm not a monster. I lift my head up and shout at Sebastian—"Let him go! Freddie is feral and rutting and just bonded an omega with bond-sickness. We cannot keep them apart. It'll kill them both."

While I'm willing to let her go right now, this is not over. She's still mine. Freddie didn't take her from me. This is temporary. Yes. His bite is shallow. Maybe they could break...no. That's dangerous. Jake, don't hurt your omega. I have other options. I always have more ways than one to get what I want.

As soon as he's free, Freddie launches at me and Ondine. I let my arms fall.

Instead of ripping my throat out, a possibility because he's a snarling feral alpha rushing his way towards me, he only goes for Ondine. And when he gets to her, he catches her before she falls. He backs away from us and takes her into a corner.

"Leave us! She's mine!" Freddie snarls with a preternatural voice.

I grab Sebastian and pull him out of the nest and shut the door.

I crash onto the floor in front of the door and rake my hands through my hair.

"Fuuuuuck!!"

We left a feral alpha alone in a nest with her! I turn to my alpha, who stands above me, and howl at him. He doesn't cower. My power and influence erupts, and my ears pop. Shit. Sabbies grabs at his ears.

Sebastian kneels down next to me. "Jake, listen to me. You need to calm down. We need to calm down. And we can't go back in there. She's his now."

I close my eyes and take a deep breath.

How did I lose her this quickly? I never even had her.

***

Ondine

I can feel him. There's a cord that ties us together, from my heart to his hands. Invisible. Magical. Unreal.

And what passes down it is all his loud emotions. Right now, his only thought is of me. *Mine. Mine. Mine. Mine.* I can practically hear him think.

Freddie has laid me bare before him and is biting me, with decisive, exacting, fiery bites from my feet on up. I think he's trying to cover every inch of me. I love it.

He's not breaking the skin, but he's leaving marks. He growls at my skin when the marks fade from my rapid healing. I giggle at him for it.

Freddie. My Freddie.

His smell is now unburied and everywhere. Earl Grey tea. Bergamot. Black tea. Orange. And this lovely olive oil quality to it.

"Kiss me," I mutter.

No one ever kisses me.

He keeps biting, and I wiggle away from him. He growls at me and pulls me back.

"Freddie, kiss me," I say louder. Can he hear my soft voice over his growling and panting?

He pauses and then lifts his head from my hip, where he just laid down another bite. "My mate wants a kiss?"

He's so beautiful. The hard lines of his face. His thin, dark lips. He has pretty eyelashes fanning over his shiny brown eyes. I want to stroke and taste and marvel at all the parts of him.

"Please. Kiss me." I say again.

He positions himself over me. His elbow on the side of my head. His hand on my jaw. "Of course, princess."

Before I can finish exhaling, he's kissing me. My being blooms open. It feels better than any kiss I've ever had. I can feel his gratitude. His lust. His desire. His love.

Love.

Is that what this is?

His tongue waves into my mouth, and my tongue meets his. Every press of our lips makes the bond between us sing.

This is wonderful.

And unexpected.

Of course, it's unexpected. I've found my phantom alpha. The man in the woods. It's been Freddie this whole time.

I deepen our kiss, wanting to consume him.

I wish I would have known earlier. Or even suspected. But I didn't think for a second that what had happened that night was real. I thought it was a fever dream from perfuming. My entire body transformed. I spent days in pain as my body grew and changed.

My boyfriend broke up with me shortly after. He texted me and asked if I wanted to go to dinner with his parents before they drove him back home. I said yes, but showed up looking like death and obviously an omega. He was mad I didn't cancel.

He was mad that I was always saying yes. Even when I shouldn't.

My friends, which I had so many at the time, didn't know what to do with me. They'd known me as a beta, like them. A few friends came over or texted, but it all just felt like a goodbye. It was bad timing anyway. Most of us had just graduated.

But none of that seems to matter now, with my alpha surrounding me. I've never felt more satisfied in my whole life than now.

Which isn't saying much, actually.

I need more.

I manage to flip positions, so I'm on top. Freddie pulls us both towards the wall, and he sits up, my knees straddling him, our chests together and upright.

"Can I fuck you?" I ask.

Freddie throws his head back in a scoff. "Please, princess, please ride me. Do what you need to do."

He's hard and ready for me. I take some time with my hand, stroking him up and down between us, watching him react to me. He's getting impatient because he sits up tall and grabs me like I weigh nothing and positions me over him. "Now," he growls.

Oh, I like impatient men, I just decided.

I drop down onto his dick, and I am so damned jealous of myself. It's a perfect, perfect fit. We both make horrendous noises. His arms wrap around me, and I lay my head on his shoulder.

Freddie doesn't fall into a crazed rut. He's not the animal he worried he'd be with me. Our hearts pump at the same beat. I move over top of him in small waves, our breaths synching, building our pleasure together.

It's a joining.

He licks his mark on my neck, sending my entire body into both a solid and liquid state. I quicken my movements on him and whimper. So he does it again. I didn't know you could do that. He licks my mark like he's tending to it. Like it's the most special thing to him.

I love my feral mate.

Our arms are both holding onto each other, wrapping us both in the vines of affection and acceptance. My mate. Mine.

Epilogue

Jake

I shut it off. I shut it all off. It's what I do when things get rough. I can switch.

What needs to happen now? That's all I need to focus on. There's no need to cycle over how we left Ondine alone with an unbonded, feral male. I've been holding back on behaving like my usual sociopathic self, but I will not let her be taken from me. I will do everything I can, everything I know how, to ensure she'll be with me.

She's mine.

Afterword

Ondine's story concludes in Vol. 2, so don't worry. Everything is going to work out...I swear.

I first published Ondine by the episode on Kindle Vella in 2024. It was a great platform to begin my publishing journey, and I made lots of lovely reader friends. Ondine was well received and loved. She was, though, an unfinished serial with 50 or so episodes when Kindle Vella shut down. The forces behind Amazon and Kindle encouraged me to release the serial as an ebook, assuring me they would get it back to my subscribers.

I chopped her in two, gave her an ending, commissioned a cover artist (the illustrious Killdera), rallied some beta readers, and put her out in the world as a bona fide ebook.

For the second edition and first paperback, Ondine needed a professional edit, so I hired Kenzie with Cupid's Inkwell to make it print ready. I cannot sing her praises enough for being the most dedicated, kind, intelligent editor a girl could ask for. Thank you, Kenzie, for your comments and your commas.

Ondine's story is so important to me. She's my air sign queen. I wanted to give her as many love stories as I could. Thank you for reading, and please enjoy the rest of the Cash City Omegaverse Stories. I've gotten a taste for writing books, and it's made me feral.

xxx Shasta

About the author

Shasta has been writing her whole life. She was an editor on her college literary magazine, where she got her Bachelor of Arts in Literature. She lives in Salt Lake City, UT with her two kids and three cats. Ondine is her first self-published novel.

www.ShastadeLeon.com